Christmas is...

Gifts are not a... hold in your hand... at Christmas is the small baby born in a stable, though the shepherds and the wise men did manage to bring presents as well.

These books also celebrate Christmas, and each deals with a different gift, the kind that can bring immeasurable love and contentment down the years—which we wish for all of you.

Enjoy!

As a person who lists her hobbies as reading, reading and reading, it was hardly suprising **Meredith Webber** fell into writing when she needed a job she could do at home. Not that anyone in the family considers it a 'real job'! She is fortunate enough to live on the Gold Coast in Queensland, Australia, as this gives her the opportunity to catch up with many other people with the same 'unreal' job when they visit the popular tourist area.

Recent titles by the same author:

MARRY ME*
LOVE ME*
TRUST ME*

Trilogy

BAUBLES, BELLS AND BOOTEES

BY
MEREDITH WEBBER

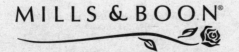

MILLS & BOON®

All the characters in this book have no existence outside the imagination
of the author, and have no relation whatsoever to anyone bearing the
same name or names. They are not even distantly inspired by any
individual known or unknown to the author, and all the incidents are
pure invention.

First published in Great Britain 2000
Harlequin Mills & Boon Limited,
Eton House, 18-24 Paradise Road, Richmond, Surrey TW9 1SR

© Meredith Webber 2000

ISBN 0 263 82278 8

Set in Times Roman 10½ on 11½ pt.
03-1200-49902

Printed and bound in Spain
by Litografía Rosés, S.A., Barcelona

PROLOGUE

'STAND up, Fran, I want to try something.'

Griff erupted into Fran's office in his usual energetic fashion, his long arms waving her to her feet. Dark silky hair flopped forward over his forehead and his blue eyes gleamed intently as he pursued some mad idea.

Knowing it was easier to obey than question, Fran stood, and was only slightly bemused as Griff circled her desk and placed his hands on her shoulders.

Bemusement changed to shock when he bent his head and kissed her on the lips. Which was when her emotional state slid into something she didn't quite know how to analyse.

Before she could get a grasp on it, he lifted his head and frowned at her.

'Come on, Franny, kiss me back. Put some effort into it!' her boss, and owner of the Summerfield Medical Practice, ordered.

She should have asked why. Or simply refused. But in the six months she'd been working for Griff, she'd discovered it was very hard to refuse him anything. The man didn't seem to understand no, and he always had a good reason why she should do whatever it was he wanted her to tackle.

Although she would never, *ever* go rock-climbing with him again. Not after the abseiling incident!

These thoughts all flashed through her head as Griff's lips again claimed hers. Not only claimed, but warmed them somehow. Made her tingle in an unfamiliar, but certainly not unpleasant manner. Especially when his tongue sneaked seductively between them and she had to catch her breath or pass out from a hazy sensation that suggested a sudden depletion of oxygen.

'There! That was much better!' Griff announced, straightening up once again and looking down at her with unmistakable satisfaction.

'Much better than what? A barium enema?' Fran demanded, as the after-shocks caused by her reaction to Griff's kiss threw her mind into chaos.

The wretch grinned at her.

'Much better than the first one, of course,' he elaborated. 'Be honest, Fran, you must admit it was OK.'

Totally bewildered now, Fran stared at her friend and colleague.

'Why should I admit anything of the kind? And what does it matter anyway? In fact, why were you kissing me at all?'

But as she asked the final question a possible answer occurred to her and she stood on tiptoe to peer more closely at his lips.

'It was a joke, right? You've wiped something revolting across your lips and later you're going to tell me that's what I've been kissing? Or you've painted on a special formula and my lips are going to go blue or swell up or do something else just as gross! Honestly, Griff...'

Her voice faltered as she shifted her attention from his lips—very shapely—to his eyes—definitely his best feature—and saw not the usual teasing laughter in the blueness but something she couldn't quite define.

Something that made her stomach feel vaguely queasy.

'Griff?'

He smiled at her and the laughter returned although he was trying hard to look hurt.

'As if I would!' he said plaintively. 'How could you think such a thing of me?'

'Easily,' she told him, and didn't bother reminding him of all the times he'd played some stupid joke on her. After all, the man had the memory of an elephant and had to know precisely why she was suspicious.

'It wasn't like that,' he protested, still doing the plaintive thing. 'It was more in the nature of an experiment. A taste test.'

'A taste test?'

Fran realised a certain amount of repetition was creeping into her part of the conversation but she couldn't stop echoing his words.

'Like a trial run,' he added helpfully, but it didn't help in the slightest as far as Fran was concerned.

'A trial run for what?' she tried.

'For marriage!' he claimed triumphantly, his smile broadening, his eyes twinkling as if this was the most marvellous of marvellous ideas—the best yet! The ultimate!

Fran sat down.

'You kissed me as a trial run for marriage?' There was the repetition thing again. 'Whose marriage? And what did kissing me have to do with it? You must know you can kiss! If Kerry Ryan's to be believed, you've been doing it since you were four when you caught her behind the azaleas at kindergarten. And I have vivid recollections of our student days, when any number of nubile young women would have testified to your skill.'

'Were they azaleas? I've often wondered what azaleas looked like.'

Fran frowned at the man who'd saved her sanity six months earlier and sighed. She'd have ground her teeth as well, only a recent visit to the dentist had impressed on her the importance of keeping her tooth enamel intact.

'Forget the azaleas, Griff, and get back to marriage,' she ordered, knowing how easily conversations with him could be sidetracked by trivia. Though why her stomach should be shifting uneasily at the thought of Griff considering marriage…

He perched on the edge of her desk and bestowed another radiant smile on her.

'I've been practically going demented, trying to work out what to get Mum for Christmas,' he began, and Fran bit her tongue, praying that, if she let him be, he'd eventually get to the point. 'I mean, she's not well enough for a trip away somewhere and, now she's got Barney coming in to do the garden, giving her a pot plant seems a bit crass. It tends to underline the fact she can't do as much as she did before, doesn't it?'

Fran nodded. Eloise Griffiths was not only her patient, but a dear and much-loved friend and mentor, and Fran's heart ached whenever she considered the older woman's increasing debility.

'And she's not reading much, so a book's no use—'

Fearing another sidetrack, Fran cut into his explanations.

'Griff, I don't want a list of all the things you're not getting for your mother for Christmas. Get to the point.'

He held out his arms in a helpless gesture.

'But that *is* the point, Franny!' he said, and Fran felt the little surge of warmth which him calling her by the softer name always generated. 'I was thinking and thinking and suddenly it struck me. There was only one thing my mother wanted from me. Really wanted! More than anything!'

His arms stretched wider—this time in a gesture that heralded great news.

'Grandchildren!'

Fran must have looked as blank as she felt for he patted her on the shoulder and added in a kindly fashion, 'Not right away, of course. There'd be a wedding first, and then the grandchildren later. She'll understand these things take time and I couldn't gift-wrap the progeny and hand them to her on the day. She'll know she'll have to wait a while but, although she never nags about it, I know it's her greatest wish and heart's desire. To see me settled down with some nice woman who'd be willing to produce a small Griffith or two.'

If anything, his smile grew brighter as he sought her approval.

'Brilliant, isn't it?'

Fran's mind fumbled for an appropriate answer. She could certainly understand the concept—and, yes, more than anything, Eloise wanted to see her son happily married—but…

'Have you decided who?' The question didn't sound right. 'I mean, this nice woman? Have you one picked out? I've been here six months and, as far as I can see, you've spent so much time with me—helping me settle in, showing me around, getting me over the wretched Richard—you haven't had time for a social life.'

A frown dimmed the sparkle in his eyes.

'Didn't that kiss mean anything to you, woman?' he demanded. 'Didn't you feel it had possibilities? Here! Let's try it again.'

And before Fran could answer—or argue against a repeat performance—he hauled her out of her chair, clamped her to his chest and once again pressed his lips firmly against hers.

Only this time his tongue did more than sneak seductively between them. It teased and tempted, it tantalised and taunted. And suddenly she found herself kissing him back.

What seemed like a century later, Fran eased herself out of his arms and slumped bonelessly back into her chair.

'So what exactly did that prove?' she asked weakly, her body now as confused as her mind had been earlier.

'That we're compatible!' he announced. 'That sex would work between us. So what about it, Franny? I know you want kids—I can tell from the look in your eyes whenever you run a clinic session.'

At the far end of the dark tunnel into which the words had plunged Fran, a faint light glimmered, although, the way she felt, it could have been the headlight of a train rushing towards her at great speed!

'Sex would work between us?' she muttered. To hell with repetition, she had to get this straight! 'You want me to have your kids?'

'Well, we could go the artificial insemination route if the idea was unsavoury to you—the sex, not the kids,' he said, 'but I kind of thought the sex part might be fun. After all, we like each other—we're great mates, always have been—and I figured if the trial kiss didn't make you throw up or anything then…'

The hesitation was only momentary, certainly not long enough for Fran to lodge a protest—even if her whirling brain had been able to think of one.

'Look at it this way, Fran. You've worked with me for six months without stabbing me with a scalpel, and we probably see far more of each other at work than a normal married couple do at home—or when they're courting, for that matter. Which proves we should be able to rub along OK in a marriage, doesn't it? Genetically we should be great—I can bring a bit of height into the mix, and you've got lovely skin to offer, to say nothing of a rare combination of blonde hair and soulful brown eyes.'

'Heaven forbid I should be genetically unsuitable!' Fran said tartly, but once again Griff didn't seem to hear.

'And my mother adores you,' he continued. 'It's perfect!'

Thinking maybe the situation would make more sense if she was upright, Fran stood up again, then realised the movement brought her dangerously close to Griff's long, lean body. Which up until the kiss had failed to arouse the slightest flutter in her breast.

She walked across to the window and looked out at what she could see of the little town of Summerfield. Her six months here had restored her health and rebuilt her confidence. The warmth and friendliness of the locals had done wonders for her battered self-esteem, and even her sense of humour was back in working order.

Or so she'd thought until this latest bombshell!

Which wasn't at all funny.

Or perhaps it was.

She turned to face the man behind her return to 'life'.

'You're joking, right?'

He shook his head.

'No way! It's the obvious solution.'

'To your dilemma over what to buy your mother for Christmas?' Fran heard the shrillness in her voice, but shrill didn't begin to cover what she was feeling.

And Griff had the nerve to smile again.

'It did begin that way,' he admitted, 'but then, when I considered it from other angles, it began to have an appeal all of its own. You know my record with women, Fran. Six weeks is a long-term relationship. I'm old enough to realise the "truly madly deeply" love thing isn't going to happen for me but, as I see it, there's more to marriage than all the randiness and pulse-accelerating stuff, which, from my observations, wear off anyway.'

Very quickly, Fran thought wryly, remembering Richard's eventual confession of repeated infidelities—beginning within two months of their marriage.

She shut away the memory as Griff continued.

'But what we've got goes beyond all that. We like each other as friends, even if we're not in love, and we'd have all the benefits of marriage. Companionship, kids, regular sex—'

'Well, that's *very* important!' Fran snapped. 'Though,

from all I've heard, it isn't nearly as regular once the kids arrive.'

'But you do want kids?' Griff persisted, as usual ignoring anything he didn't wish to hear. 'You've said as much. Told me you regretted giving in to Richard's demands that you wait a while, although you were glad they weren't around to be hurt by the divorce.'

He must have taken her stunned reaction to this justification as encouragement, for he smiled again and spread his arms wide.

'Well, what do you say?'

CHAPTER ONE

FRAN'S happy bubble of marital delight burst twelve months later, at exactly eleven minutes past five on Tuesday, 29 November. True, she'd had twinges of concern, slight nudges of conscience, not to mention an escalating level of guilt that she wasn't fulfilling her side of their marriage bargain, but until that moment—

'I've always put it down to normal period pain,' Laura Kenton, her final patient for the day, was saying. 'I can remember, as a teenager, my mother telling me she'd always suffered badly. Then last week I read this article about endometriosis—it talked about the terrible cramps, the same symptoms I have, and about doctors rarely diagnosing it.'

As Fran listened, she realised it could have been herself talking. She could even hear her mother's voice ringing in her ears. 'A lot of women have bad period pains. It could even have been genetic, something you got from your birth mother—like your brains.'

Surely not! she told herself, yet deep inside, where the coldness of dread was already taking hold, doubt was coalescing into certainty.

'But the article didn't say much about what causes it or what to do about it,' Laura continued. 'It was slanted more towards how few women actually sought medical advice for the symptoms, accepting them as normal in their particular case.'

Fran set aside the personal revelation—and its unwelcome implications—to concentrate on her patient.

'Endometriosis is hard to diagnose because the symptoms can be so diverse,' she explained. 'Some sufferers don't have cramps at all, some have back pain, some find intercourse uncomfortable—but there's no definitive test that can isolate it.'

'Why not?' Laura demanded. 'If doctors can detect a number of cancers from a patient's blood these days, why not sort this out as easily?'

Fran did a quick mental scan of what she knew about the disease, seeking a simple explanation to a very complicated problem. One she'd have preferred not to be considering right now.

'It's not something that shows up in the blood because it's not like a systemic infection or an invasive disease. What happens is that uterine tissue—made up of the cells lining your uterus—strays to other parts of the body. In some cases to the ovaries or Fallopian tubes, or to the intestines.'

She omitted the rarer and scarier cases where tissue had been found in the lining of the nose, even in the brain. Right now she was having trouble speaking normally as she pictured her own Fallopian tubes blocked solid by endometrial scarring. The eggs she needed to produce the children Griff wanted—the children for which he'd married her—queued up in the tubes, useless, imprisoned by the idiosyncrasies of the disease...

'The problem is that this tissue, not harmful in itself, behaves exactly like other uterine tissue, swelling then breaking down at monthly intervals. However, unlike the ordinary menstrual fluid which drains away, the blood from the rogue cells in other parts of your body is trapped and causes irritation to the tissues surrounding it.'

'So, if I've some of these cells in my nose, it will bleed every month?' Laura asked, and Fran, in the midst of her private panic and despair, found a small smile tweaking at her lips. So much for not mentioning noses!

'Exactly,' she replied.

'I suppose I can be thankful for small mercies,' Laura joked while Fran struggled to keep her private persona and her professional self separated.

'Is there any good news?' her patient asked.

'It can be treated,' Fran assured her. 'By drugs or by surgery.'

She saw Laura's frown and hurried on.

'A physical examination may suggest a problem, especially if the problem is in the lower abdomen, but laparoscopy—inserting a thin tube with a light and telescopic lens through a small hole in the abdomen—is really the only way of telling if you do have it, and how widespread it is. And during laparoscopy the surgeon can often laser out any wandering tissue he finds, so it can be a cure as well as an investigation.'

'Often?' Laura echoed.

'In more severe cases open abdominal surgery might be required, but there's no need to leap ahead to that possibility until we know more.'

She thought of cases where damage had been so severe both ovaries had had to be removed—and shuddered. No doubt that's what had happened to her. Given the physical symptoms she'd always suffered—and accepted as normal—it was the logical explanation for her failure to conceive. A failure which had been casting a long shadow on her happiness in recent months.

'So, can you do this or do I have to go to town?' Laura's question cut across Fran's silent self-diagnostic review.

She studied her patient for a moment.

'No to me doing it. It's a specialist procedure. And as for town, although Jeff Jervis is a very good obstetrician and gynaecologist, I don't know that he has either the experience or the equipment. It may mean a trip to Toowoomba.'

Mentally, she was booking herself in as well—as soon as possible—although heaven knew what excuse she'd give Griff. Her stomach somersaulted at the thought of the man she'd unwittingly grown to love. If Griff found out...

Perhaps she wouldn't book herself in. After all, what was the point? By the time she had treatment, tried again to conceive...

'I'll talk to Jeff. He'll recommend someone if he can't do it,' she told Laura, once again putting her own escalating anguish to one side and forcing herself to concentrate on her patient. 'Do you want me to make the arrangements for you? Would any time suit you?'

Laura beamed at her.

'Would you? Take any appointment you can get. I'm not working at the moment. I know there's always a long waiting list to see specialists but if you could pull strings...' She blushed prettily, then added, 'I'd really like to get it sorted out. I'm getting married in a couple of months and I'd rather have everything fixed up first if I possibly could.'

Fran knew exactly how she felt. There was no way she'd have agreed to Griff's daft proposal if she'd had any inkling...

'If I have this lap-whatever, how will it affect me? Affect having sex and children and all that stuff?'

Laura had asked another question Fran hadn't wanted to hear.

'With the drugs used to treat the disease, there's a long delay—six to nine months of treatment and then perhaps another three months before ovulation occurs naturally.'

And another nine months after that? No way could she consider it, given Griff's hopes and Eloise's health. And considering his proposal had been inextricably linked to her producing Griffith offspring, adoption wasn't an option.

The final words repeated themselves like a taunting dirge

in her subconscious while she forced her conscious mind back to the problem in front of her.

'Because you're young, it's unlikely the disease is wide-spread. With laparoscopy, everything should be back to normal in a fortnight. If you had to have open abdominal surgery, the recovery time would be about four to six weeks.' She paused, knowing in her own case she'd de-layed too long already—that she should have considered this as a reason for not falling pregnant six months ago!

Given her age, a diagnosis six *years* ago would have been even better. Six years ago she'd only have been a little older than Laura was now. Six years ago maybe the scarring wouldn't have been so severe…

'I'll see what I can do and let you know,' she promised Laura, as she made a final note on the young woman's file and stood up to see her out. She walked her patient to the door, reassured her again that she'd be in touch, then leant on the jamb and watched the young woman walk away.

'Are you finished? Ready to go home?'

Griff's voice made her turn. He'd had an afternoon of minor surgery, and was still wearing his short white coat. It made his skin look more tanned, his hair darker, his eyes bluer.

Her heartbeat faltered into an uncertain rhythm, as if not sure it should be showing its usual quickening to the man, then accelerated anyway—involuntary muscle doing its own thing.

'I've a few phone calls to make, notes to write up, things to check.'

She was aware of offering too many excuses but she needed time to think this through and just lately, since she'd diagnosed another personal problem—a case of lovesick-ness—thought had become impossible with Griff around.

He smiled, and her heart forgot its uncertainty and went

into bounding-leap-of-happiness mode—undeterred by her mental warnings of restraint.

'We're in separate cars so I'll see you later, then. I'll call in on Mum, and pinch some of the new snow peas Barney's growing up there. We can have them with our dinner. I'll cook.'

Such a simple domestic exchange! Fran thought to herself, backing into her office so she didn't miss a final glimpse of Griff. Almost like a real marriage.

Only it wasn't a real marriage, no matter how it might seem to her.

She shut the door and slumped against it.

He'd married her for one reason and had been quite open and honest about it. He wanted grandchildren for his mother. Grandchildren Eloise Griffiths could enjoy before the heart disease that sapped her energy and drained her spirit eventually took her life.

And Fran had agreed—in part because it had been easier than saying no to Griff, but also because it had suited her needs as well. He'd been right to think she wanted children—right about them getting on together as well. What she hadn't expected had been to fall in love with him. Hopelessly and irrevocably in love.

Which hadn't been a real problem up until today.

Months ago, when the realisation that she loved the man had finally sunk in, she'd considered the implications rationally and carefully. She'd accepted that Griff didn't love her in quite the same way she now loved him, but he seemed happy enough—and their sex life was great.

She'd eventually decided that, providing she kept her feelings under wraps and didn't put Griff under pressure by demanding or expecting reciprocal love from him, the marriage could go on as it had begun.

But what if she couldn't keep her part of the bargain?

What if she couldn't physically produce the children he wanted?

It wasn't fair to keep him tied to her.

Her head answered the question she hadn't wanted to ask, while her heart, which had become a reliable if uncomfortable barometer of her feelings, grew heavy. She sighed as she slumped into her chair behind the desk and pulled out the small notebook with the phone numbers of all the specialists they used in town.

Half an hour later she had an appointment organised for Laura with a specialist in Toowoomba, the large regional city beyond town. She'd again considered making an appointment for herself but knew it was already too late. With Eloise's health failing, Fran had more important things to do than confirm what was more a certainty than a suspicion.

She had to extricate herself from her marriage, ease her way out so Griff could marry someone else—someone who *could* bear his children.

That had to be her first priority.

A tear dropped onto her desk as she realised that anything beyond that was so far down the list it didn't matter.

Fran stood under the shower two mornings later and considered her options. The day had brought new confirmation of her failure to conceive and, although her cycle had always been irregular, today's slight evidence strengthened her determination to release Griff from any obligation to her.

And while a sneaky voice inside her suggested she wait until she'd seen a specialist, rather than push ahead on the strength of her belated self-diagnosis, she'd spent long sleepless hours weighing up the symptoms she'd had for years, and knew the specialist's opinion wasn't necessary.

Besides, she'd already wasted too many days and weeks and months of Eloise's limited life, selfishly enjoying the unexpected bliss of falling in love with Griff—the warmth of being part of his family. Now it was time to make amends.

Most importantly, she had to keep any hint of her own problem—not to mention her heartache—from him. He was too soft-hearted, too much of a gentleman, to let her divorce him for practical reasons, no matter how desperately he wanted a child.

'Hey! What happened to our conservation campaign? Aren't we still on a ''save water, share a shower'' kick?'

The object of Fran's gloomy thoughts, tall, dark and impossibly handsome, appeared first as a fuzzy shadow beyond the patterned shower curtain, the random movements of his limbs suggesting he was flinging off his pyjamas as he spoke. Then he was beside her, clasping her wet body firmly to his as he adjusted the taps to suit himself.

'Ouch! That's far too hot,' Fran told him, telling herself at the same time that she should get out. Get dressed. Keep away from him while she worked out how and where to begin the extrication business.

Unfortunately her body, the cause of *all* her problems now she considered it, betrayed her yet again, seeming to find its position against Griff's too comfortable to forgo.

'I've got to get moving,' she muttered feebly. 'I promised your mother I'd look in on her before work, and you've got a meeting at the council chambers about the immunisation programme so I'll have to take the early drop-in patients.'

Griff, of course, took absolutely no notice of this reasoned argument and continued to nibble at the skin behind her left ear—a procedure that made shivers run up her legs and her toes curl in a kind of painful bliss.

Determined to ignore the delicious sensations, which she suspected were but a prelude to what he had in mind, she turned towards him and got the full force of the shower in her face—just as she drew breath to repeat her objection to the dalliance.

She spluttered and choked, and Griff switched immediately from sexy seducer to concerned spouse.

'Are you sure you're OK?' he asked, wrapping her in one of the big bath sheets they favoured, then patting her anxiously on the back.

'I will be,' she promised. 'Just as soon as I get my breath back. You finish your shower.'

He let her be, which was just as well because, the way she was feeling, any more sympathy would probably have had her weeping in his arms.

She'd never wept in front of Griff, but Richard had hated women crying. Melodramatic nonsense, he'd always said it was. Turned on to get their own way.

She shivered at the memory of the tears she'd hidden from her first husband then realised, with the kind of wonderment she'd come to accept as part of her life since she'd remarried, that she'd never had reason to cry with Griff.

Until now.

And that wasn't Griff's fault.

He joined her in the kitchen as she fixed the bowl of cereal and fruit that constituted her breakfast.

'Chicken feed,' he said, shuddering theatrically to express his disapproval of her taste.

'Fat fiend,' she retorted, taking refuge from her despair in their customary breakfast exchange of insults over each other's food choices.

He dropped two pieces of bread into the toaster and turned on the griller. As he passed her on his way to the refrigerator for the cheese he would slice onto his toast then grill until it was golden brown, he touched her lightly on the head.

'Mrs Miller might be in early. She's been having problems with bursitis in her shoulder and wants a cortisone injection. I suggested she might like to try an anti-inflammatory drug. See if that works first.'

Fran nodded. Mrs Miller was a relative newcomer to the town, a glamorous widow in her early forties. Both Fran and Griff suspected she phoned her former GP for advice before each visit to the surgery, as she always offered suggestions for her treatment.

'And I'll call in on Mum—that will save you one chore,' Griff added.

Fran raised her head and looked directly at him, her insides turning mushy with the love that had hit her as unexpectedly as summer flu. Only this was a far more virulent infection, burning in her blood, ineradicable and all-consuming.

The object of her affection, blissfully unaware of her state, continued to fix his breakfast.

Unrequited love!

Those dismal two words, the saddest of all phrases, rang in Fran's head.

'Calling in on Eloise is never a chore,' she said, because it was expected of her—and she meant it—but also because it hid the deep stab of regret her thoughts had triggered.

'Nonetheless I'll do it. That way you can dally over your chicken feed, read the paper, relax a little before the sick of Summerfield besiege you with their problems.'

He retrieved his cheesy toast from the griller, cut each slice into three fingers, poured coffee from the pot Fran had brewed for him and settled at the table opposite her.

He lifted his cup towards her.

'Here's cheers!'

Fran touched her orange juice to the cup and repeated the toast, but her heart wasn't in the silly little ritual. In fact, it was so heavy with unhappiness she wondered how she'd carry it through another day.

'If the council agrees to fund the immunisation programme, will you want to start it before Christmas?'

She asked the question to divert her gloomy thoughts, but as she heard her own words she realised it was something else to take into account. Professionally, she couldn't leave Griff in the lurch, right when he was taking on extra work.

'I think we should. It's not a particularly happy thought, but at the moment there's a heightened awareness of the dangers of not being protected against disease. Fleur's death is still in the forefront of people's minds.'

'Such an unnecessary tragedy!' Fran muttered crossly, as the anger she'd felt when the diphtheria outbreak had swept through the small town resurfaced.

'It was a sign of the times,' Griff reminded her. 'In recent years there's been a big upswing in people not getting their kids immunised. It grew out of the back-to-nature thing, like whole foods—whatever they may be—and organic gardening. Towns like Summerfield attracted people who wanted an alternative lifestyle, so it's not surprising there's a disproportionate number of kids not immunised.'

'I don't know how you can make excuses for them when they've put other children, and elderly people, at risk. This country went for years without a diphtheria outbreak, and now it's popping up all over the place.'

'People are entitled to their own opinions as far as the health of their children is concerned,' Griff said mildly, and Fran scowled at him.

'You know your problem? You're too nice!' She pushed her chair back from the table and stood up, wanting a fight—wanting to yell and rant and rave to relieve some of the tension knotted inside her body. 'Too willing to see the other person's point of view.'

Griff looked up at her.

'Is that what's bothering you? My niceness?'

Fran's hand froze on the glass she was lifting. She'd been so careful to hide her deepening despair from Griff—so certain she'd been carrying on quite normally.

'Bothering me? There's nothing bothering me.' She told the lie quietly, hoping it might not count if it was barely audible. She turned towards the sink at the same time so he couldn't see her face and read her dismay. 'Did Mrs Miller make an appointment?'

Nice, safe medical talk, but would Griff run with it?

She waited, gripping the sink, aware of the internal knots getting tighter.

'No. I bumped into her at the supermarket yesterday evening and explained the "come early and wait" system.'

Fran eased her fingers from their clamped position, checking to see if she'd left indentations so fierce had her grip been.

'I wouldn't have put her down as either the "come early" or the "wait" type,' she said lightly. 'More a "languishing in bed until mid-morning" personality. And last time I saw her, I was running all of five minutes behind and she told me her previous doctor never kept her waiting.'

She rinsed her bowl and glass and set them on the draining rack, her body moving through a familiar routine while her mind darted and dodged, raced and hesitated, fussing away at a problem that wasn't going to go away.

'I'll see you later,' she said, and, because she always did it, she dropped a kiss on the top of his head, pressing her lips against his thatch of thick, dark hair.

Griff watched her walk out of the kitchen. She'd clean her teeth, smooth some cream onto her clear, lightly tanned skin, add a touch of palest pink lipstick to her full, tempting lips, then run a brush once again through her long silky fair hair before twisting it in some miraculous way to the top of her head and securing it with two pins.

His body tightened and he sighed.

He knew the position of those two pins—and how easily he could remove them. He knew the faint perfume of the cream she would use and the taste of the pale pink lipstick. He also knew her favourite foods, her taste in music and how to please her in bed, but after eleven and a half months of marriage he still had absolutely no idea what went on inside her lovely head.

What she thought and how she felt—particularly what she thought and how she felt about their marriage—was a complete mystery to him.

He sighed again, finished his toast, washed his dishes and placed them in the draining rack, then went to visit his mother.

'Am I too nice?' he demanded, bending to kiss his maternal relative's cheek. She was sitting on her wide verandah, giving orders to Barney who was now in charge of her extensive, formally structured garden.

'I've always equated nice with boring and I couldn't ever pin that label on you,' his mother assured him. 'Do you think I should have white or blue petunias along that border?'

'White looks cool in summer,' Griff replied, then realised that, in responding to his mother's query when he'd rather have pursued his own problem, he was being nice again.

Perhaps he'd answered his own question?

He stayed for half an hour, their conversation dodging between health and garden issues while his mind played with the four-letter word his wife had flung at him earlier.

Fran drove the short distance between the house and the surgery. Everywhere in Summerfield was a short distance and she'd have preferred to walk, but if an emergency call from an outlying farm came in she'd need the car.

She parked outside the neat brick building that housed

the practice, and sighed. Once inside, she'd have to be pleasant, caring, efficient and definitely in control. The fact that she felt none of these attributes only made it harder to pretend.

Harder to get out of the car, to walk inside, greet Meg— their receptionist—and smile!

The smile would probably be the most difficult part of the act, so she practised one in the rear-view mirror.

Not a good look. Perhaps today she could stick with serious.

'Have you and Griff decided which of you is going to Toowoomba for the rural medicine conference?' Meg didn't look up from her computer screen, apparently divining who had entered from the footsteps. 'I have to reply, although I guess if you don't mind a unisex thing, just plain ''Dr Griffiths'' on your name tag, I wouldn't have to give a name and you could keep arguing about it.'

'We haven't been arguing—' Fran began, but the denial was enough to divert Meg, who turned towards her and cocked an eyebrow.

'Not a real argument,' Fran finished feebly. 'Griff thinks I need a break—that I might be getting stale—but as I keep telling him, it's years since he had time away. Before I came he couldn't get away, but now he's got no excuse.'

'If you hadn't rushed your wedding, we could have arranged a locum and you could both have had a holiday,' Meg pointed out, then she grinned lasciviously. 'If you count a honeymoon as a holiday!'

Not wanting to think about her wedding—a riotous afternoon of fun and laughter to which the whole town had been invited—Fran made a noncommittal noise and lifted the pile of patient files from the counter.

Then she remembered she had good reason to want to go to Toowoomba. Endometriosis needed treatment even if she wasn't going to have children.

'Put my name down for it,' she said. 'That will save any further debate.'

Meg nodded, then waved her hand towards the files Fran was clutching.

'Mrs Miller's coming in shortly. She particularly asked for Griff, but I explained he wouldn't be in. Then she wanted an appointment with him later in the day, but he's booked out.'

'She could have come tomorrow,' Fran muttered as she walked away, glad of an excuse to be grouchy.

When she'd first arrived in Summerfield, she'd realised that all the patients preferred to go to Griff, whom they knew and undoubtedly loved. But gradually she'd weaned enough of them away from him to both ease his load and boost her own confidence in her ability as a GP. Though a few more patients like Mrs Miller could cause that to waver.

Not that it would matter soon!

The heart-barometer did a lurching kind of thing, but Fran ignored it, focussing her mind on work. Besides, Mrs Miller's all-too-obvious preference for Griff had given her an inkling of an idea, reminded her just how popular Griff had been with women in their student days!

She had time to flick quickly through the files, reading newly arrived lab reports and specialist letters. Nothing in Mr Cable's blood to explain his symptoms of dizziness and vertigo. Jane Ewings's most recent check-up with her oncologist showed her breast cancer still in remission—no sign of any rogue cells settling in anywhere.

The phone interrupted her progress.

Meg's voice.

'Mrs Miller's here—shall I send her in?'

As Fran agreed, she tipped the pile of perused files back up the other way so Mrs Miller's was on top. The last time this patient been in, she'd seen Griff for a 'bunion' on her big toe, which Griff in his notes had 'callously' described as a 'small callus'.

Fran smiled to herself and stood up to greet the patient, who, at eight in the morning, was well enough dressed to have fitted right in with the elegant crowd at a big race meeting. In laid-back Summerfield, her appearance was verging on the ridiculous.

'Griff tells me you're having pain in your shoulder. Is it the left or right?'

Having greeted the woman, waved her to a chair and learned it was the right shoulder, Fran walked around her desk.

'Have you had it before?' she asked, running her hands over the woman's neck and shoulder, feeling for any obvious swelling or irregularity.

'No, but I used to get tennis elbow and a cortisone injection would fix that so I know it would fix my shoulder.'

Fran moved to stand in front of her.

'Lift your arm like this,' she instructed, demonstrating the movement she wanted Mrs Miller to make. 'And this.'

She worked through the range of movement, but none showed any restriction. Nor did her patient's face reveal the wince of pain she would have expected at some stage of the test.

'When does it hurt?' she asked.

'When I do this,' Mrs Miller told her, and proceeded to lift her arm with her elbow bent and her hand sliding behind her head to touch her left shoulder. 'It's part of my exercise programme.'

Fran found she was the one wincing.

'That's more of a stretch,' she said cautiously. 'Do you do it regularly?'

'Every morning,' Mrs Miller told her. 'At six. There's an exercise programme on the TV that I follow. As you get older your skin and muscles lose their elasticity, but with regular exercise you can slow down the effects of age.'

She recited it as if she'd learned it by rote, but Fran was impressed in spite of herself. She was also aware of a faint tingle of uneasiness somewhere in the back of her mind. Too faint to identify, unfortunately.

'I admire you, being able to exercise like that. It takes real dedication and commitment to keep going, day in and day out,' she said. 'Where does it hurt when you do that movement?'

An elegantly manicured finger, tipped with the vivid red of fresh blood, indicated not the shoulder joint but the trapezius muscle where it stranded up towards its anchoring point at the base of the skull.

'In there,' Mrs Miller told her.

Fran slipped back into her chair and pulled out a laminated chart showing the posterior view of the human muscular system. Then she picked up a plastic model of a hip joint.

'Do you know how bursitis happens?' she began, and when her patient shrugged a negative reply she continued.

'The bursae are little sacs of fibrous tissue between tendons and the bones beneath those tendons. When you move your joints, the bursae secrete fluid and act as little cushions so the tendons move easily across the bone. For any number of reasons, including exercise, strain, arthritis, or trauma, these bursae can become inflamed—and movement of the affected area becomes very painful.'

'My shoulder's hurting all the time,' Mrs Miller told her. 'Not just when I move.'

Fran nodded.

'But higher up,' she said. 'In the muscle. I think it's muscle strain, not a joint problem.' She felt her own trapezius. 'Is it sore to touch? Up here?'

Mrs Miller prodded dutifully and this time the wince was obvious.

'Will cortisone fix it?' she asked, and Fran had to hide a smile.

For some reason, many patients these days expected there to be a pill, potion or injection to immediately alleviate their symptoms.

'Rest it for forty-eight hours and use an ice-pack on it—a few ice-cubes wrapped in a face washer will do—a couple of times a day. That should help both the pain and the healing.' She thought for a minute, hoping the tingle of uneasiness might have turned into something more definite. No such luck! 'And when it's feeling better and you begin your stretches again, don't push too hard, ease that muscle back into work. Don't overdo it.'

She used her 'that's all I can do for you today' voice but Mrs Miller didn't budge.

The tingle returned.

'Was there something else you wanted to discuss?' Fran asked, searching the woman's handsome features for some sign, some indication, that she was troubled.

She might just as well have searched a picture in a magazine for all she learned. Mrs Miller's dark eyes looked back at her, perhaps seeking answers in Fran's face.

'I'll try the ice,' she said, when the silence was becoming uncomfortable, then she added, 'You haven't been here long, have you?'

'Eighteen months.' As Fran replied she had a glimmer of an idea. 'And, no, I'm not counted as a local yet. I think it takes at least twenty years—maybe longer—although I've always been made to feel welcome and people couldn't have been kinder. Not all small towns are so accommodating.'

Mrs Miller shrugged.

'I'm not looking to be made welcome,' she said abruptly, and on that note she rose to her elegantly shod feet and walked towards the door.

CHAPTER TWO

FRAN was so surprised by the remark it took her a moment to realise her patient was leaving. She shot out of her chair and hurried after her, too late to open the door but in time to call goodbye as Mrs Miller strode down the short passage, through the reception room and out the front door.

'And what did you say to upset her ladyship?' Meg asked when Fran's bewildered state brought her to a halt beside the front desk.

Her ladyship!

'Do people treat her like that?' Fran asked the receptionist. 'Like someone a bit above them? Do you think she's having trouble settling in? That she's unhappy here?'

'If you go around like you're better than everyone else, then people will have a bit of fun at your expense.' Meg pointed out the obvious. 'Not to her face, of course. But she doesn't work, and she hasn't joined in anything, doesn't go to the Country Women's Association meetings or church or even bingo, so folks are bound to wonder why she came to Summerfield, aren't they?'

Fran thought of her own precipitate arrival in the town.

'Perhaps she was unhappy wherever she was,' she suggested, a glimmer of fellow-feeling aligning her to the cool, aloof woman.

'Yes, but why Summerfield?' Meg persisted. 'You came because Griff went off to Toowoomba and dragged you back here. And a good thing you did. He was going to kill himself, trying to run the practice on his own once the town began to grow.'

She didn't add that it had been a good thing for Fran as

32

well, although Fran had realised very soon after her arrival that the entire town had known some version of her marriage break-up and her own subsequent decline into a robot-like creature who had lost her zest for living and her joy in laughter.

'No other early patients?' She spoke to change the subject as it was quite obvious there was no one awaiting her attention.

'It's pension day,' Meg reminded her, and Fran chuckled, remembering how surprised she'd been when Griff had first pointed out the phenomenon of no one ever needing medical attention early on pension day. Shopping was the first priority every second Thursday, and even later in the day appointments were always fewer. 'But Mr Cable will be here at nine. I think he makes appointments on pension day to get him out of pushing Mrs Cable's trolley.'

'Thanks for reminding me,' Fran said. 'I want to look up a couple of books, see if I can track down a possible cause for his dizzy spells.'

She walked back to her room, but her mind was on Mrs Miller not the elderly but still spritely Mr Cable.

Why *had* she come to Summerfield?

If she was looking for a new husband, surely a city would offer more scope than a small country town. And she was far too old for Griff, past child-bearing age, although—

Fran was barely back at her desk when the phone buzzed.

'We spoke too soon about it being quiet,' Meg informed her. 'Accident at the school. Two kids collided. Mrs Moreton wondered if you could pop down. She doesn't want to move them.'

Fran's heart did a panic squeeze this time, although she told herself that Mrs Moreton, the primary school headmistress, was sensible enough to have phoned the ambulance for a real emergency.

Perhaps it was a real emergency! The ambulance was pulling up as Fran drove into the car park. An older child, obviously designated as guide, pointed to the infants' playground, and Fran, bag in hand, headed that way.

'Let me know what you need,' Alan Gibbs, the ambulance attendant, called after her.

Alan was conscientious enough, and good at his job, but he was what Griff described as a conserver of sweat. Not one to go rushing about if it didn't prove necessary.

'I'm sorry to have you racing down here,' Jackie Moreton greeted her, 'but these two silly rabbits ran into each other, playing some wild game, and knocked each other silly. I wouldn't have panicked but Roslyn, who was on playground duty, said they both lost consciousness, Ross only momentarily but young Peter was out of it for a minute.'

The two 'silly rabbits' were lying on the ground, wrapped in blankets, their injured heads resting on pillows.

'They can move their hands and feet so there's no spinal injury, and their tongues aren't affected either,' Jackie added.

Peter Drake, familiar to Fran from his regular visits to the surgery for other accident-related traumas, already had a decent-sized bump rising on his forehead.

'I went subconscious,' he announced to Fran.

'Unconscious,' she corrected automatically as she checked his pupils and felt for his pulse.

'What's subconscious, then?' he asked.

'That's when something inside you tells you racing round and round the tree is stupid,' Jackie told him.

'Is that what you were doing?' Fran asked, more to test his memory of the event than because she wanted to know.

'Not just racing,' Peter told her. 'We were charging— like with electricity—which is why we had to go different ways.'

'Peter said we *had* to,' Ross complained. 'He's always telling me what to do.'

'You don't have to obey him, surely,' Fran said, turning her attention to the smaller, paler child. 'Does your head hurt? Which bit of it bumped against Peter's?'

Ross lifted his hand and touched the side of his head just above the ear. Fran felt the area, although she knew it was unlikely the bump had caused damage to the skull. She checked the reaction of their pupils to light, asked a few more questions, then stood up. The older student was hovering at the edge of the shade and Fran sent her off to tell the ambulance attendant he wouldn't be needed.

'They're both OK,' she said to Jackie, 'but they should rest up for the day. I know Peter's mother works—can you keep him at school?'

Jackie nodded.

'With so many mothers working these days, we're set up for that kind of thing. In fact, I have a couch in my office so I can keep an eye on "sickies". Ross's grandmother will take him. She usually has him after school on a Thursday anyway, as his mother goes to town.'

Fran smiled at the word. 'Town' was eighty kilometres away, not far yet considered by the locals to be an outing of great importance. 'Town' had competing supermarkets, and a 'twin' cinema which ran movies throughout the day. Going to town was special.

She repeated her warning about the children resting, adding that if the condition of either should change—if they should show signs of drowsiness or slurring of their speech—to contact her immediately.

'Drowsiness?' Jackie echoed. 'Shouldn't they sleep it off?'

'At eight-thirty in the morning it's not natural for small boys to be sleeping, so it would be better if they could look at books, or colour in, or do something to pass the time.

Drowsiness could be a sign of more damage than we can pinpoint at this stage.'

'I'll tell Mrs Jessup to keep an eye on Ross,' Jackie promised, then she knelt beside the boys.

'OK, you two. Up to my office, but walking quietly, no running, and no horsing around, you hear?'

She spoke firmly but her hands as she helped the little fellows to their feet were gentle and Fran felt a sense of loss—and a longing so deep it startled her.

Unwilling to acknowledge it, she bent and gathered up the pillows and discarded blankets. She'd been hoping to conceive to please Griff and his mother, she reminded herself. Just because she enjoyed children in her work, that didn't mean…

'Peter's so intelligent it's hard to keep him occupied,' Jackie was saying as they followed the boys towards the building, while Fran's mind puzzled over her reaction to the boys. 'And if I can't come up with something before too long he'll be labelled a troublemaker, a label that will follow him through school, and all that potential will go to waste.'

The thought was sufficiently startling to grasp Fran's wandering attention.

'Why label him? How can his potential go to waste?' she asked, as Jackie waved Peter to the couch in her office, and indicated to Ross to sit in the chair in front of her desk.

'A really bright child in a class is as much trouble as the child who doesn't want to learn,' Jackie explained quietly, while she checked a ledger then dialled a phone number. 'The bright child grasps concepts much more quickly so the repetition of lessons, which the bulk of the children need to instil something into their heads, is boring for him. And because he's bored, he starts playing up—teasing other kids, finding mischief of some kind to keep him occupied.'

'He starts to drive his teacher mad, hence the trouble-maker tag,' Fran said. 'So what's the answer?'

'Letting him proceed at his own pace. Setting challenges for him. Feeding his need to learn more.' Jackie sighed. 'Not easy when there are twenty-five other kids in the class to be taught, and supervised, and challenged in a different way.'

'You have computers. Aren't there programmes for more gifted children he could work on?'

Jackie glanced towards the couch where Peter had settled himself and was now absorbed in tracing the triangles in the geometric pattern of the material covering it.

'Unsupervised, he'd probably take the computer apart. He's fascinated with how things work, though I haven't a clue what he's picked up about generating electricity that had he and Ross pounding around that tree.'

'Turbines?' Fran suggested faintly. 'I'm afraid my knowledge of electricity is confined to how to press down on the switch to make it work.'

'Me, too,' Jackie agreed. 'Well, I'd better sort things out here. Thanks for coming.'

Fran made her way back to her car, her mind now on Jackie's problems rather than her own. What Jackie had said about mothers working had sparked another thought. Mothers had been the traditional helpers at schools—there for the tuck shop, listening to reading, providing support on sports days or outings—but now students like Peter, who needed special supervision at times, were missing out.

Though surely, in a town like Summerfield, there were enough mentally active adults with time on their hands to help an intelligent little boy reach his full potential.

For a start, there was Mrs Miller...

She found it easier to think about Mrs Miller than about her own problems right now, although she knew she didn't have the luxury of time.

*   *   *

'Tea for two coming right up! Or does bringing it to you, rather than letting you get it yourself, qualify as "nice"?'

Fran felt an inner cringe as Griff accosted her in the passage outside her office. It was mid-morning and she'd been seeing Jane Ewings out and checking she had a break before the next patient.

Griff's tone suggested he'd taken 'nice' as an insult— which she'd probably intended it to be—but in her present state of confusion she didn't know how to apologise.

Although putting a little distance between them—offering the odd insult—might not be a bad idea.

'Jane OK?' Griff continued, as if he hadn't expected a reply. He hovered, tray in hand, waiting for her to precede him back into her room. 'Tests showing she's still in remission?'

'Yes—all clear. So far so good. I'm sure it's helped that she's been so positive throughout the whole business.'

Fran tried to focus her mind on the patient who'd just departed—not easy with Griff in the room.

Before she'd married him—before she'd been so foolish as to fall in love with him then realised she'd had a problem—she'd enjoyed the moments they'd snatched from an often hectic schedule to sit down and drink a cup of tea together. They'd discussed patients, debated possible treatments, generally shared information, giving each other the kind of back-up which had made the job easier, and their services to their patients more comprehensive.

'Is she still on a three months' schedule?'

Griff's question reminded her that, for him, nothing had changed.

'She's just had the final three-month appointment. Her specialist has told her he doesn't want to see her for six months, although I've suggested she might want to keep the monthly appointments with me.'

Griff nodded.

'That gives her a security blanket if she thinks she needs one—and it leaves it up to her to cancel if she's feeling strong enough to stand alone.'

Fran sipped at her tea. A security blanket! It was a peculiarly apt description of what Griff had provided for her when she'd first come to Summerfield. But falling in love with him had stripped it away, and had left her vulnerable and confused.

Especially now the certainty that she had endometriosis made it impossible for her to continue the charade. Yet even as her stomach did a downward pitch to register her despair, she understood it was important to pretend everything was normal.

'Did you have any luck with the immunisation programme?' she asked, noting the way his long eyelashes shaded his eyes as he drank his tea. Sealing the image in her mind like a miser hoarding gold.

'As far as council funding is concerned, it was yes to infants and children, no to adults—although if we can get the funds elsewhere or if people are willing to pay for their own boosters, we can use the facilities at the town hall to carry it out.'

Fran smiled.

'That would certainly be easier than having the entire town troop through the surgery. What's the next step?'

Griff studied her face for a moment, then glanced at his watch.

'I'll have a patient waiting by now. What if I tell you over lunch? Let's play hookey. Go down to Patty's Pie Shop for some of her delicious asparagus quiche?'

The thought of food made Fran feel slightly ill, but when she looked at her husband she knew she couldn't refuse.

Fun sparked in his eyes like sunlight glinting off the sea, and Fran was seduced into smiling. This was Griff's gift—

an ability to invest something as simple as a lunch date at the local café with all the excitement of a major event.

'See you at one?' he pursued, standing up then bending to retrieve the teacups.

'Or thereabouts,' Fran agreed, telling herself at the same time that lunch with the man wasn't unusual enough for stomach jitters. After all, they lunched together almost every day, and breakfasted together, dined together, slept…

It had to stop!

Immediately.

And she had to work out a plan that would ease her out of both their marriage and their partnership at work without causing Griff any unnecessary hardship.

Now!

The urgency of the situation struck home so unexpectedly she didn't stand to greet the next patient who came tentatively through the half-open door.

'Are you ready for me?' Mrs Granger asked, her voice more timid than usual—if that was possible.

Fran shot to her feet.

'Of course I am. I'm sorry, I was dreaming.'

She dashed around the desk and helped support the elderly woman as she abandoned her walking frame and eased herself into the chair.

'How have you been feeling? Less pain on the new tablets or no difference?'

Mrs Granger's faded eyes stared up at her, a blueness around the irises testifying to her age.

'I didn't take them,' Mrs Granger announced. 'My pain's not so bad, and it doesn't seem to get worse or better whether I take tablets or not.'

Fran leant back against her desk.

'So you don't need a new prescription today?' she surmised. 'Is there something else troubling you?'

Mrs Granger was the most uncomplaining of patients, so

a visit for something other than a repeat prescription for her anti-inflammatory tablets was rare.

She shook her head, causing sparse grey hair to flutter in the ensuing draft.

'I will need a new prescription for the tablets,' she replied. 'Though not right away.'

Fran bit her tongue. Sometimes silence worked better than questions.

'It's for Maddie. I've been giving her the tablets. She's actually much older than me so it stands to reason her arthritis is worse.'

Maddie? Fran searched her mind for an elderly patient of that name—and for a reason the woman wouldn't have her own medication.

'With dog years you multiply by seven, so it would make her one hundred and five and I'm only ninety-five, you know.'

Fran did know! Not only knew but worried about it. Ninety-five was a fair age and, although Mrs Granger insisted she could manage on her own and refused to accept even a service as non-intrusive as meals-on-wheels, Fran fretted over it.

Now there was a dog to worry about as well!

'How do you know Maddie needs the tablets?' she asked, then realised it was the wrong question. In fact, she shouldn't be asking questions at all. She should be suggesting that Mrs Granger take Maddie to the vet, pointing out that drugs which worked for humans might be harmful to dogs.

No, she couldn't worry Mrs Granger like that!

The old lady was explaining how Maddie no longer jumped to catch a ball, and how her back legs seemed stiff when she woke in the morning.

'Just like mine,' Mrs Granger declared. 'Until I dropped

one of my tablets and she ate it and seemed better in the morning, although she's still not jumping to catch the ball.'

'At one hundred and five I might not want to jump to catch balls,' Fran said soothingly, while her mind pondered the problem of prescribing for dogs.

If Mrs Granger hadn't told her what was going on...

'You had a repeat on the script I gave you,' she said, although ethically she was sure she should be saying something else.

Mrs Granger beamed at her.

'Yes, and I've already had it made up. But I wondered if you'd look it up in that book Dr Griffiths has about all the drugs and let me know if it could be harmful to a dog. If I should perhaps give her half instead of the whole.'

Fran smiled.

'Why don't I check it out and let you know?' she said. 'I'll call in this evening on my way home from work.'

Mrs Granger nodded her approval of this decision and began to struggle out of the chair. Fran helped her, then held her elbow until she'd steadied herself on the wheeled frame.

'I'll see you later.'

Mrs Granger tottered off, Fran keeping an eye on her until she'd safely negotiated the sliding door at the front of the building.

Despite Mrs Granger's faith in Griff's drug book, Fran knew nothing they kept in their library would describe the effect of human drugs on dogs. She smiled to welcome her next patient and made a mental note to phone the vet.

'There's not much difference in the make-up of animal and human drugs,' Ian Sinclair, the local vet, told her much later in the day when her final patient had departed and she caught him as he finished his afternoon session. 'We tend to prescribe more on a weight basis, so many grams per kilo, but ask Griff about Mrs Robertson some time.'

'So what she's been giving the dog wouldn't hurt it?'

Ian hesitated.

'Give me the dosage again,' he said, and Fran read out the dosage and the ingredients.

'Maddie's a grossly overweight basset hound,' Ian explained. 'She probably weighs more than Mrs Granger so the body weight ratio wouldn't be a problem.'

'And ethically?' Fran said to him, because she knew this was why *she* was worrying.

'Hard one, Fran,' Ian told her. 'The problem is, while Mrs Granger knows I'd see Maddie for nothing because I know she can't afford my fees, her pride won't let her come to me and not pay. Then you have a further dilemma because if she buys a similar animal drug for Maddie it will cost considerably more than the subsidised tablets she buys for herself.'

'Gee, thanks for pointing all that out!' Fran said dryly, and smiled as she heard Ian chuckle.

'Joys of small-town practice,' he reminded her. 'We all know each other far too well for there to be any easy options. And speaking of small towns, are you and Griff going to the firefighters' Christmas shindig?'

'Of course,' Fran said, but the smile she'd worn earlier faded. A week ago—in fact, a few days ago—she'd been looking forward to the end-of-year dinner-dance organised to raise money for the local volunteer firefighting unit. It was one of the big social events of the year in Summerfield and she'd gone so far as to take a trip to town to buy a new dress.

Now...

Although...

'Well, I'll see you there if not before, and let me know what you decide about Mrs Granger and Maddie. I could probably rustle up some samples of the drugs, but that's a short-term solution.'

'If only she hadn't told me,' Fran muttered, but her mind was again drifting off her patient as the germ of an idea Mrs Miller's visit had planted earlier began to take shape in the dim recesses of her brain.

Leaving Griff was one thing—after all, he wasn't in love with her so he'd be more inconvenienced, perhaps put out, than deeply hurt. But he'd taken so long to get married in the first place, he was hardly likely to rush into marriage a second time no matter how desperate he was for children.

Perhaps if she…

Would it work?

Could she make it work?

She ignored the cold despair invading her body, concentrating instead on likely candidates.

After all, wasn't love about making sacrifices?

Didn't loving someone mean you put their needs ahead of your own?

'Ready?'

The subject of both her mental plotting and physical pain stuck his head through the door.

She stared at him, trying to see him as a stranger might—wondering why it had taken her so long to fall in love with him. Why she'd chosen Richard in the first place when both fellow students had asked her out.

'To go home? Little place just down the road. Remember home?' he teased, and the accompanying smile caused a tightness in her chest.

'I've a house call to make, so you go on ahead,' she said.

A momentary inward twitch of his eyebrows was as close as Griff got to frowning, and she saw the movement now. She'd also seen it earlier when she'd pleaded being behind in her paperwork to avoid going out to lunch with him. But she needed time apart from him at the moment—not increased togetherness.

'I won't be long,' she promised. 'And it's my turn to cook and to take any calls, so you can have a shower, sit down and enjoy a long cool beer.'

He looked at her for a moment longer, no doubt remembering why it was her turn to take the calls—because he'd decided she'd looked tired, and had insisted she take it easy over the weekend while he did Saturday's two-hour surgery session and fielded the emergency calls.

'I'll see you shortly, then,' he said, and disappeared from view. It wasn't until later that Fran realised he hadn't asked which patient she was visiting.

Neither had she volunteered it.

Their easy exchange of information was breaking down—another sign, surely, that she had to end the farce.

Griff drove home, telling himself it was foolish to be worried just because Fran had cancelled lunch—no big deal—and hadn't said which patient she was visiting after work. In a town the size of Summerfield, he could hardly follow her to see who it was. Doctor spies on wife!

Nor could he ask about the phone call—the one she'd had earlier, when he'd walked past her room and seen her smiling more happily than she'd smiled for ages, although it had only been in the last two days he'd sensed she'd withdrawn even further.

Guilt that he'd hustled her into marriage began to gnaw at his intestines, yet he'd been so certain, at the time, it had been the best thing for both of them.

Still was—surely. For his part, he was frequently surprised at just how much he enjoyed being married, having Fran around as a permanent fixture in his life.

Very comfortable.

Or it had been, until recently, when he'd begun to wonder if it was as eminently satisfying for Fran as it was for him.

*   *   *

'So tell me how you plan to run the immunisation pro-gramme?' the cause of his concern demanded, arriving home as he settled himself into his favourite chair, icy low-alcohol beer frosting the glass on the table by his side.

'Are you going to sit down and relax while I talk?'

She grinned at his question.

'No, but I will let my hair down,' she said, removing those tantalising pins so the shiny waves tumbled around her shoulders. 'Grilled chicken and salad OK for you for dinner?'

Fran dug a brush from her handbag as she spoke, and when he'd agreed on the menu she disappeared into the small powder room beneath the stairs where she'd brush her hair, tie it back from her face with a coloured band, then have a wash and emerge refreshed and ready to tackle the next task. Their dinner.

'Will Nev Crooks give you free publicity in the *Summerfield News* or would you have to pay for a publicity campaign?'

Her interest was so apparent that Griff forgot his gloomy suspicions and put forth his few tentative ideas.

'I thought I'd ask Nev if he'd print an article on the dangers of not being immunised. I could bring in the num-ber of deaths in Russia during the outbreaks in 1996 and 1997, and mention that adults who haven't had boosters since they were young children could also be at risk.'

He picked up his beer and crossed to the divider between the living room and big country-style kitchen. Fran had her head in the refrigerator, but even her rear view was attrac-tive. Of medium height and very slim, she had an uncon-scious kind of grace he never tired of watching, while her body—

'And an ad running underneath the article to say boosters will be available for children and adults on such-and-such a date?' She straightened and swung to face him as she spoke, a head of lettuce and a couple of tomatoes balanced in one hand, a cucumber and two celery stalks in the other. 'Will you mention cost?'

She dropped her selection into the sink, bending slightly. He sometimes thought, in his more fanciful moments, they could have been moulded to the right specifications for each other's contours, so comfortably did they fit together.

'Do you think it might scare people off?' she continued when he didn't answer. 'Could we ask one of the service clubs to sponsor it—perhaps subsidise the cost of the vaccine so it's really cheap? Maybe one of the medical supply companies would donate the needles.'

He dragged his thoughts off how well her body fitted to his—and steadfastly ignored the physical reaction the thought had caused. Switched back to business.

'Sponsorships are a great idea, but in a town this size, where the same limited number of people are called on to sponsor or give to all the equally deserving causes, it's not likely we'd succeed. Trying the medical companies might be more fruitful—and perhaps the state government for a subsidy of some kind.'

'If they went dollar for dollar with the local council—' Fran began, then she broke off to answer the phone.

He watched her, waiting to see if it was business, feeling again a jab of discomfort when he saw her eyes sparkle as she smiled, then heard her husky chuckle as she said, 'No, Ian. It was nothing like that.'

The rest of the conversation caused even more disquiet, consisting of Fran saying, 'No, he's here,' which Griff assumed was in response to a question about his own whereabouts, then a series of more negatives, each one more determined than its forerunner.

'That was Ian Sinclair,' she said—unnecessarily, Griff thought—when the conversation finished and she returned to putting together salad ingredients.

Griff waited for her to elaborate, to explain why the vet—single and very good-looking—would be phoning her. But not a word did she offer, tracking back instead to their previous conversation and infuriating him by her apparent lack of conscience over whatever secret she and Ian Sinclair shared.

Not that he could let her see how aggravated he was. Or how curious. He drained his beer and was about to walk around the divider to get himself a second when she fore-stalled him by reaching into the refrigerator and passing him another cold can.

'I don't think I'll have another,' he said, releasing some of his ire in petty stubbornness. 'Perhaps a glass of wine with dinner. You might join me. One glass won't affect your work or your driving.'

Not that she would, he thought grumpily. She'd never have even half a glass when she was on call, something he'd had more reason to admire than denigrate until tonight.

'So, what did Ian want?'

The question, coming as it did in the middle of a con-versation about booster shots, seemed to startle her, but as it had startled Griff as well—he'd been *determined* not to ask—that seemed fair.

'He wondered if we were going to the firefighters' dance,' Fran replied, and Griff imagined he could see faint colour in her cheeks while an evasive quality in her voice betrayed the lie.

'You seemed to be saying no more often than you said yes,' Griff pointed out, his uneasiness increasing as his wife's behaviour led him into hitherto uncharted regions. 'We are going, aren't we?'

Now she flashed a smile at him.

'Of course,' she said, bestowing on him a faint echo of that earlier chuckle. 'I've been to town!'

She slapped the chicken breasts with the flat blade of the

big butcher's knife she favoured, then sprinkled chilli and pepper flakes on them.

'Ian's sister will be staying with him at the time. She's a nurse and between jobs at the moment.' There was a pause, then Fran added in an inconsequential tone, 'Single, too.' But her fierce and totally unnecessary concentration on two bits of chicken flesh gave the game away.

Though why Ian having a single sister should affect them...

'Perhaps we should make up a party. Help raise funds by bringing friends along?' Fran added.

Griff nodded his agreement but the words didn't mean much.

There was something brewing in that lovely head of hers.

Something more than making up a party for the firefighters' dance.

Something he didn't think he'd fancy.

And if it involved Ian Sinclair...

Griff found his hunger abating, and a heat that felt like anger building in its place. With a mammoth effort, he turned the conversation back to the immunisation programme.

'Did you know scientists somewhere overseas are working on a genetically engineered banana that could provide necessary vaccines orally?'

The concept was so startling that Fran forgot her heartache and the fledgling 'plan', to query him.

'We could eat a banana instead of getting booster shots? How do you find out these things? I swear I read all the same magazines as you.'

He grinned at her and she decided maybe the plan wasn't such a good idea after all—no matter how much she loved him and should be willing to sacrifice.

'Women's minds work differently. You probably retain

information from the articles that goes immediately out of my head, but things like bananas stick with me.'

'Because it's food,' she teased, but inside she felt her heartache return. This easy companionship might be comfortable for Griff, but it wasn't why he'd married her.

Back to the plan!

CHAPTER THREE

NOT that planning was easy, even though it was based on common sense. The way Fran saw it, Griff would be more likely to accept her leaving their marriage if there was someone he fancied in the offing.

Someone with whom he'd fallen instantly in love would be the ideal, but surely, Fran told herself, the fates wouldn't insist on *that* great a sacrifice!

Rather than relying on one candidate, she decided she'd need three or four.

Over the weekend, with Griff busy helping a farming friend dip his cattle, she phoned dozens of friends and acquaintances and, using the pretext of updating her Christmas card list, sought out the current relationship status of women she knew or had known even slightly.

Preferably younger women.

'I don't care how desperate your local firefighters are to make money,' her best friend Louise told her, 'you shouldn't ask Billie Firth. Can't you remember how besotted Griff was over her? He went out with her for longer than he did with any other of his other women, then she decided to marry Bill Lloyd instead, probably because their names matched.'

Billie Lloyd, née Firth, now divorced from Bill, went to the top of Fran's list. As a doctor, with training in general practice work, she would be ideal.

Fran felt the twist of pain in her chest, and forcibly reminded herself that this was for the best—that she owed it to Griff because of all he'd done for her. Her heart could ache as much as it liked, and her stomach stay jittery, but

51

she was going to sort things out for the man she loved if it was the last thing she did!

'My cousin, Josie—you know, the one who models— well, she's back in town and would love to meet some clean-living country men.' Her second-best friend, Sheila, offered Josie, and Fran snapped her up.

'We'd come ourselves,' Sheila added, 'but this latest baby's due any day and I refuse to appear in public when my breasts are four sizes larger and Dan makes remarks about how his father would have liked a herd of milkers as good as me.'

In spite of the sadness of regret that now clouded Fran's life, she chuckled at the image. She'd heard Dan say those exact words after Sheila had produced her first infant.

'Tell Josie if she's got free time she's welcome to stay on,' Fran told Sheila. 'As long as she likes.'

Closer to home, there were a couple of single teachers at the primary school. Fran had heard one of them was all but engaged to a high-school teacher in town, but 'all but' wasn't settled. That particular young woman was dark and Griff had always had a penchant for dark-haired beauties. And any woman with eyes in her head and even half a brain would see that Griff was better marriage material than the absent school teacher.

She phoned Billie Lloyd and managed not to gag while the woman gushed her delight at being included—even offering to make an outright donation as well as buying a ticket.

'But I don't want to intrude on you and Griff,' Billie added. 'Isn't there a fairly classy B & B just outside Summerfield? I'm certain I saw a write-up of it in *Gourmet Traveller*.'

Chastising herself for her overwhelming sense of relief, Fran agreed to make a booking for Billie at Chatsworth.

By the end of the day she had five on her list, counting

both teachers. To be fair, she'd have to ask a couple of young men to even things out. The smaller and weedier the better! And Ian's sister—Ian could come, he'd help balance the numbers—Billie and Josie.

Would it do?

Was five enough of a choice to offer a man who'd taken out dozens of women in his time?

Should she keep trying?

'You've done what?' Griff bellowed when she broke the news of the house-party to him on Sunday evening. 'Don't you have enough on your plate, working full time and running the house, looking in on my mother every day, caring for half the town one way or another, without adding more work for yourself with a whole heap of people we barely know staying here?'

She must have looked startled by his reaction—which she was. Griff never bellowed. He rarely raised his voice! Next minute he was by her side on the couch, his arm around her shoulders.

'I'm sorry, Franny,' he added gently. 'But I've been worried about you. You've been looking tired lately. Why take on this extra hassle?'

His arm tucked her up against his body, and she felt his warmth feeding into her coldness. The treacherous thought that if she did nothing this could go on drifted across her mind, but she batted it away. She owed Griff too much to betray him in such a way.

She eased herself off the couch. Out of touching distance.

'You said yourself it's hard to raise money for all the services in the town because it's the same people giving all the time. I thought if we included some outsiders in the various fund-raising activities, we might relieve the pressure on the locals.'

'Typical female logic!' Griff growled. 'Now it's my fault

you're going to run yourself ragged entertaining all these people.'

'It's not "all these people", and hardly "entertaining",' Fran countered. 'All I'm suggesting is a pre-dinner drink at our place before going on to the dance. Punch and nibbles, beer for the men, nothing fancy at all.'

He shrugged his wide shoulders and lifted his hands in an I give in gesture.

'If it makes you happy…'

It makes me want to cry, she could have said as she turned away from him, crossing to the small telephone table to find a notepad and pencil. She knew the only way she'd be able to handle the next few weeks was by keeping busy. Organising the party would be a start.

Getting back to other work-related issues was something else she had to do—it was important to tie up any loose ends. There was the problem of Peter Drake and the provision of challenges for his intelligence. Which brought Mrs Miller to mind. Her increasingly frequent visits to the surgery—always to see Griff—were a worry. Fran didn't want Griff attracted to Mrs Miller—who might be good-looking, but was at the very upper end of her child-bearing years.

'Is the notepad biting you that you're looking so fierce?'

Griff's question arrowed through her muddle of half-thoughts and ideas.

'There's s-so much t-to do,' she stuttered, looking first at the inoffensive notebook, then up at her husband. 'Before—' She bit off the words that had nearly slipped out.

'Before the party?'

She shook her head, anxious to play down any effort less he demand she cancel it.

'The party as you call it, will be a few people here for drinks. It's no bother,' she said.

But would he let it go?

Oh, no!

'Before Christmas?' he persisted, standing up and coming to put his arm around her shoulders—warming her body again! 'Is that the problem? Look, I know you offered to have Mum and the aunts here for Christmas this year, but you don't *have* to do it. Mum would be just as happy for all of us to go out. The pub puts on a very fancy Christmas dinner. She and I took the aunts there the year before you came when it was our turn to do the dinner.'

Fran was about to deny her concerns had anything to do with Christmas, which last year had been celebrated at Eloise's sisters' home, when she realised Griff had provided her with the perfect excuse.

'No, I'll do Christmas dinner here,' she said. After all, she could hardly leave him before the celebrations. New Year—that's when she'd go! January brought its own promise of new beginnings and it was a good time for a new doctor to settle in. The surgery was quiet during the summer holiday month when many families headed for homes or flats at the beach. 'It's no trouble.'

Again she eased away from Griff's casual embrace. To cover her escape, she began to scribble furiously in the notebook, as if planning the impromptu drinks was taking all of her attention.

Actually, having remembered Peter Drake, and Jackie's prediction about his future, guilt at not doing something about it earlier had superseded both the plan and the party in her mind.

'What does Mrs Miller do all day?' she asked Griff, then couldn't resist adding, 'When she's not visiting you.'

Perhaps hurt by her second withdrawal from him, he'd settled back down on the couch, but even before she'd asked the question she'd known he was watching her. Studying her?

She studied him in turn, seeing the gravity in his blue

eyes, the way the light caught and highlighted the strands of silver in his dark hair.

'Why the sudden interest in Mrs Miller?' he asked.

'It's not so much Mrs Miller as Peter Drake,' she said. As Griff's eyebrows rose, she realised she wasn't explaining too well.

Choosing a chair rather than the too-close-for-comfort couch, she sat down and tucked her feet up under her skirt.

'You know I was called to the school—'

'It will probably be a regular occurrence while Peter's there,' Griff told her, and she had to smile at the understanding in his voice.

'But it's because he's so bright he's always in trouble,' she said, and went on to explain Jackie's concern and the dangers inherent in labelling children.

'If I could think of someone, or a number of someones, with time to spare, who'd be willing to supervise him while he works at his own pace, especially with the computer programmes the school can access,' she continued, 'it might stop any problems with his behaviour before they start—or before they become habitual.'

She looked hopefully at Griff. After all, it was his deeper local knowledge she'd been relying on when she'd first considered finding a support person for Peter.

'Isn't it up to the school to find its own helpers?' he asked.

Fran shrugged.

'I got the impression Jackie had already tried. Then I realised our patient spread covers all the town, not just the people in contact with the school. Surely there are older folk in the community who could spare a morning a week.' She hesitated, then added, 'I thought of Mrs Miller. When I saw her last week, she said something that made me think she might be feeling a bit out of place in Summerfield.'

'*Not* Mrs Miller,' Griff said firmly. 'But you're right.

There are people in town who could probably help. Mr Cable would be one. He's not only computer literate, he's also connected to the internet and knows ways to access the most amazing information. Mavis Richards would be another. Since you talked her into having surgery for her cataracts, and she can see again, it's as if she's taken on a new lease of life. She's been looking for a new interest.'

Fran filed the names away, intending to call Jackie in the morning, but part of her mind worried at Griff's first sentence. His very definite statement, 'Not Mrs Miller.'

She unfurled her legs and leaned forward, hoping Griff's concerns were medical, not personal. Though she knew it shouldn't matter to her.

'Why not Mrs Miller?'

She saw the hesitation in his eyes, and read evasion into his reply.

'I doubt she'd be interested and I'm sure Jackie would agree that having an unenthusiastic support person would be worse than having no one.'

'I suppose so.'

Fran pretended to agree, but his insistence puzzled her. Or was it simply because she was doing some plotting of her own that she sought out hidden meanings behind Griff's words or attitude?

'Coming up to bed?'

Lost in a tangle of guilt and suspicion, it took Fran a moment to process the question. And when she did, it was to wonder how long she could keep her husband at arm's length.

'I'll be up shortly,' she said. 'I want to jot down some ideas, and phone a few people about the party.'

Suspicion was like infection, Griff decided as he made his way up to the bedroom. One small prick, and it festered away beneath the skin until it was either treated, lanced or erupted on its own. And while he certainly didn't really suspect that his wife was having an affair with Ian Sinclair, there was something wrong with Fran. She was wearing the haunted look which had so distressed him when he'd seen her in Toowoomba not long after her divorce.

If he didn't know for a fact that she wasn't pregnant, he would have put her mood swings and marked air of detachment down to the hormonal changes that went on in the first months of gestation. And while he guessed she was concerned that she hadn't yet conceived, he certainly wasn't pressuring her about it. In fact, he was secretly relieved she hadn't fallen pregnant straight away. It had given them time to settle into marriage, to consolidate their relationship.

He sighed, then slumped down on the side of the bed to pull off his boots. Fran hated him sitting on the pretty bed cover because it creased easily, but she didn't ever nag about it—preferring to get into the room first so she could remove it before he arrived.

He smiled to himself, pleased he'd learned to see through her little strategies. Pleased she bothered with them rather than nagging! In fact, up until recently, she'd been the perfect wife.

He stood up, took off the bed cover, folded it as he'd seen her do, then sat down again.

The perfect wife!

The week began like any other. Breakfast rituals complete, they drove to work together, discussing other possible support people to work with Peter at the school.

'Will you phone Jackie before approaching these people, or do it the other way around?' Griff asked, as they pulled up outside the surgery.

'I'll talk to her—make sure she's happy for me to be doing this,' Fran told him. 'In fact, if I've got any spare time today I might walk down to the school. I wanted to see Rob Barry as well.'

She spoke so casually that Griff guessed she assumed he knew why she'd want to see the new young—and single— teacher. Yet for some reason his gut had twisted as she'd said the name—much the same way it had when she'd laughed with Ian Sinclair on the phone.

Was he getting paranoid?

Becoming an overly possessive husband?

He hoped not, having seen women patients driven to divorce by men like that!

But as he unlocked the surgery door and held it open while his increasingly confusing wife slipped inside, he had to tell himself very firmly that checking her appointments— even switching some of his patients to her to fill up her day—would be an intrusion of the worst kind. Unethical. Ridiculous.

Tempting!

'So I doubt he would do right now, though he might be available later.'

And not listening to what she was saying wouldn't endear him to her either.

'Sorry, Fran, I missed that.' He hoped he sounded more together than he felt. He picked up the bundle of mail from just inside the door and dropped it on the top of the reception counter, hoping she'd assume his perusal of it explained his inattention.

'Mr Cable. I haven't been able to find any explanation for the dizzy spells he's been suffering. I've suggested he go to Paul Schofield in town for an MRI.'

Fran's explanation made sense this time. Griff pulled an envelope from the Rural Medicine Association out of the pile and held it in his hand as he asked, 'Are you thinking acoustic neuroma?'

'It would be one explanation,' Fran told him. 'There's

no sign of infection, and his blood tests are all clear. When I did a hearing test on him last week, there was some loss of hearing in his left ear but there's no tinnitus, or so he tells me when I've asked about him hearing noises in his ears. I'm sure if it was Ménière's he'd have some kind of tinkling or ringing in his ears.'

Griff nodded. Fran's thoroughness—or possibly her persistence to get an answer to patients' problems—always pleased him because he worked that way himself. It might be time-consuming, but if only once in a lifetime of work you saved a patient extra suffering it was worthwhile.

'If Jackie OK's the idea—or should I say when,' he amended, knowing no teacher was going to turn down an offer of help, 'I'll think of a few other people you might like to approach.'

He tore open the envelope and bent to retrieve the name tag that spilled out.

'I thought this was a reminder about the seminar,' he muttered, as the significance of a plastic card reading Dr Frances Griffiths registered in his mind. 'It's a confirmation. Look, all the guff about the programme and turning off your mobile phone—conference etiquette. Did you know Meg had put your name in?'

Was it because he was so disconcerted that he noticed Fran flinch? Or had her recent behaviour, and his own unworthy suspicions, sharpened his perceptions?

'Meg mentioned it again last week. The day you had the meeting at the council chambers. I said I'd go to stop the argument.'

The explanation was too glib by far.

'It was hardly an argument,' he said, and heard the stiffness in his voice.

Fran shrugged her slim shoulders.

'If you'd rather go, we can change the name badge.'

'I don't want to go,' he snapped, as his restraint stretched to breaking point. 'But it would have been nice to be consulted.'

And with that parting barb he stormed off to his room where he slumped into his chair and considered the fact that he and Fran might actually be fighting.

He was certainly angry. In fact, given his druthers, he'd like to smash something, and stamp his feet, and demand to know what was going on, why she was avoiding his caresses, making arrangements like this party—and going to Toowoomba on her own.

A slight tap on the door heralded her arrival, and her pale face made him wish he hadn't yelled. But if he'd expected an apology, he was doomed for disappointment. She simply dropped the rest of the mail on his desk and walked out.

Fran ached to say something—anything—to make things right between them again, but her common sense told her this was good. Disagreements with her might make the alternative selection of women she intended offering her husband seem more attractive.

Meg arrived as she crossed the hallway to her own room, and with her Janet, their nurse, and young Susie, the part-time typist who came in to help Meg.

'Mrs Miller's just pulling up outside,' Meg called to her. 'Is she seeing you or Griff?'

'I haven't checked my book,' Fran responded, 'but I guess it's Griff.'

And you don't care, she reminded herself, though her heart knew that for a lie.

She made her way to her desk and sat down. Pieces of paper fluttered into the air, and she grabbed at them, smiling sadly to herself when she remembered how Griff had teased her about her erratic bookkeeping system.

'For someone who takes such pride in the house being neat and tidy, your note system is unbelievable,' he'd said one day when she'd shuffled through the papers in search of a note she'd made about a new drug trial.

Now the note that came to hand had 'Ask Griff about Mrs Robertson' scrawled across it, although she couldn't place a patient of that name, or remember why she had to question Griff.

Perhaps she'd better try keeping a diary again.

'Here are your files and Mrs Granger's here. She hasn't an appointment but says she'll only keep you a minute.'

Meg dropped the pile of folders on Fran's desk.

'Send her in,' Fran told her, and she stood up to meet and greet the elderly woman.

'So, how's Maddie?' she asked, when Mrs Granger had rolled her walker to a halt beside the desk and waved her hand to indicate she wouldn't sit down.

'That's what I came to tell you,' she whispered to Fran. 'My son Bill came to visit at the weekend, and I told him about Maddie getting old and her arthritis being bad, and you know what he did?'

Mrs Granger sounded both indignant and excited, so Fran didn't hazard a guess.

'He gave me money to have her put down! Imagine that! And her still full of life.'

Fran made what she hoped were appropriate noises, although Mrs Granger didn't seem as shocked or upset as Fran would have expected her to be.

'It was quite a lot of money,' the patient added confidentially. 'And as he'd given it to me for Maddie, I thought that's how I'd use it. I'll go to young Mr Sinclair and get dog arthritis tablets rather than giving her mine.'

Fran smiled.

'That's a great idea,' she said, pleased because it released her from the ethical dilemma of continuing to prescribe tablets she knew were going to a dog. 'But don't take hers in mistake for yours,' she warned.

Mrs Granger chuckled.

'Like Mrs Robertson and the heart pills,' she said, and Fran remembered her note.

'That's the second time someone's mentioned Mrs Robertson. What's the story?'

'You ask Griff,' Mrs Granger told her, turning her frame around and pushing it slowly towards the door.

Fran saw her out, and greeted her next patient. The new week was under way.

Susie brought in morning tea—no sign of Griff, no pleasant interlude. At lunchtime, Fran walked across the road and down the lane to see Jackie at the school. Griff would think she was avoiding him because of his outburst earlier and she had no intention of disabusing him of that idea.

Though she wouldn't want him feeling guilty.

Jackie was delighted about getting outside help, and Fran returned to work, knowing she'd need to talk to Griff about possible contacts yet putting it off for the moment. Where tapping on his door and walking into his office had caused excited heart flutterings in the past, now the mere thought of seeing him caused panic.

In the end he came to her, tapping on her door—but not walking in.

'I've asked Meg and Janet to stay on after work—we need to talk about the vaccination programme.'

The coolness in his voice suggested he was still upset, but an after-work meeting was good. It put off the moment when there'd be just the two of them and the awkwardness of some degree of reconciliation.

'We're getting close to Christmas, so let's try to do it all at once. Three evenings next week—Tuesday, Wednesday and Thursday,' Meg suggested, when they were settled in the small conference room, cool drinks in hand. 'Most of the newborns are being immunised on schedule so you won't have many of them. And by offering evenings, people who work can come along for booster shots.'

'But who knows if they need a booster?' Janet asked. 'What about the people who had all their shots when they were young? Surely they don't need anything now.'

'Not true,' Griff told her. 'The shots most people had as infants would have been triple antigen, which includes diphtheria, whooping cough and tetanus, plus oral polio vaccine, and probably when they were toddlers, measles and mumps—rubella for the young girls.'

'Measles, mumps, rubella and whooping-cough vaccines should all provide lifelong immunity.' Fran took up the explanation. 'But diphtheria and tetanus—and polio for that matter—are only really safe for ten years. Most teenagers are given a boost of Sabin oral polio vaccine through school health programmes, and most kids have tetanus shots to cover them if they've suffered open wounds.'

'Which leaves us all vulnerable to diphtheria should an outbreak occur,' Janet put in. 'Or all of those townsfolk who don't work for Griff, who insists on keeping track of our immunisation status and sticking us with needles at the drop of a hat.'

'People working in health care are more at risk than others,' Griff reminded her. 'And if you weren't such a baby about it, it wouldn't be a big deal.'

'If you didn't get such sadistic pleasure from sticking needles into people—' Janet began, but Meg held up her hand.

'OK, children, that's enough. I want to get home to dinner tonight and don't have time for a Griffiths-Warner battle.'

Fran found herself smiling in spite of her unhappy heart. Janet and Griff were second cousins who'd developed arguing into an art form when they'd been children. Tales of epic verbal battles had passed into the town's folklore.

Then another thought occurred to her and she studied their feisty nurse. Janet was a good-looking woman, a year or two younger than Griff. Did the arguments cover deeper feeling? Janet had married young, had still been married when Fran had first come to town. She'd shed her husband soon after Fran arrived, and had come to work for them when their dual workload became too much for Meg to handle as a sole nurse-receptionist.

And she had a couple of young children—ready-made grandchildren for Eloise to practise on while she waited...

'Is there smut on my nose? A love-bite on my neck?'

Fran felt her cheeks heat as she realised she'd been staring.

'I'm sorry, Janet. I wasn't actually looking at you, but staring in that direction while I thought of something else.' She stumbled into the apology then realised no one was listening.

'And who might have been giving you love-bites?'

Griff and Meg made a chorus of the question and it was Janet's turn to blush.

'Jerry's back in town. We're talking.' She spoke softly, but something in her voice told Fran to delete her from the list.

'Talking doesn't give you love-bites,' Griff teased, and he grabbed at Fran and pulled her close as if to demonstrate exactly how they came about.

She stiffened at the contact, not wanting his body seducing hers, even in fun. He must have felt her reaction, for his hand dropped away and his voice was as bleak as winter rain when he called the meeting back to order.

'Evenings are good—more people can attend. And giving a choice of three nights means families can juggle babysitting. I agree we go straight into it next week before school breaks up and people start drifting off for the holidays. Meg, you can handle the order for extra supplies. Now, how do we convince people they need the booster?'

'Remind them of the outbreak we had in winter,' Janet suggested, quickly enough for Fran to think she was pleased to get off the subject of love-bites. 'Remind them of Fleur. In fact, you could ask her mother if we could use a photo.'

'Wouldn't that dump another load of guilt on Mrs Foster?' Fran asked. 'Hasn't she suffered enough?'

'She's the one who opted not to immunise her children,' Meg said bluntly. 'It's people like her who are behind the recurrence of outbreaks.'

'That's true enough,' Griff agreed, 'but Fran's also right. It would be cruel to punish her by making Fleur the focus of a campaign. I think the child's death is still in everyone's mind without it being hammered home to them.'

'We can't force people to immunise either themselves or their children—all we can do is offer the service,' Janet said. 'I think if we can get the local paper to publicise it, let people know it's free for infants and children but there'll be a small charge for adults—'

'Could we make it a town effort?' Fran suggested. 'Appeal to the town spirit like the council does with the Tidy Towns competition? Use a slogan of some kind, like "Let's keep Summerfield disease free". Would that work? Would people do it for each other?'

Again she felt the sadness of regret, knowing Summerfield—disease-free or otherwise—wouldn't be *her* town for much longer.

'Great idea,' Janet said. 'That's just the kind of crazy thing that does work in this town. Especially if we can say something like, "Help make Summerfield the first town in the state to be totally prepared."'

'Hey—hold up here,' Griff said. 'We're not promising miracles. While we can offer blanket coverage of vaccinations for infants and children, I think we can limit the adult boosters to diphtheria, and possibly tetanus to anyone we'd consider at risk.'

'But we could run an awareness campaign at the same time,' Fran said. 'Let people know what other vaccines are available, and who would benefit by having them.'

'Good thinking,' Janet said. 'Griff could write a couple of articles for the paper.'

'Griff could do it?' Griff protested. 'What about Fran doing it? After all, it was her idea.'

'Oh, she'll be far too busy, organising the party,' Janet said brightly, and Fran knew the look of astonishment on Griff's face would be mirrored on her own.

'The party?' she managed, unable to believe that word of her very preliminary arrangements—for a very small select group—could have already spread through the town.

'Jill Walters is Mikey's teacher. She told me about it this morning,' Janet said blithely. 'I was telling Meg you'd probably do up the invitations on the computer after work tonight and post them out tomorrow. After all, there's less than a fortnight to go before the big night.'

Fran opened her mouth but as no words came out she closed it again.

Griff seemed equally floored—why wouldn't he be? Fortunately Meg took their silence as a signal to depart and she wound things up with a quick summary of what had been decided.

'I'll get on to the drug companies about the order and possible sponsorship and I'll also speak to the mayor tomorrow,' she promised. 'He'll love the healthy town idea and will help promote it.'

'Perhaps he could promote the party while he's at it,' Griff muttered, but Janet was now arguing with Meg over something, so only Fran heard the comment.

Which was just as well, considering the level of venom in Griff's usually cheerful voice.

CHAPTER FOUR

THERE was no escape. They'd driven to work together so Fran was doomed to be a captive audience to Griff's anger on the drive home.

Unless she stayed behind to type up invitations…

But to whom?

'A few people in for pre-dinner drinks!' he muttered at her as he opened the car door for her.

She turned to look into his eyes, unable to bear the strain between them a moment longer.

'That's all I intended, Griff,' she pleaded, hoping her tone would underline the truth of her words. 'I was as shocked by this "party" thing as you were.'

Hard blue eyes scanned her face, but whatever he read there didn't help. The hardness remained.

'Well, you're stuck with it now. Janet and Meg obviously expect to be invited, and if you ask them you can't leave Susie out. Then there's…'

He went on to list all their work-related contacts, his farmer friend, a couple of cousins and half the town council.

Fran's plan was dissolving before her very eyes. Sheer numbers would diminish the opportunity for Griff to be attracted to one of her chosen women. And he'd be obliged to do more hostly things and have no time for dalliance.

'But that's most of the town,' she wailed.

'You started it,' he reminded her, his voice as cool as his eyes.

Unable to argue, Fran slumped down into the seat and fumbled for her seat belt. Griff had already caught the strap and he passed it to her. As their fingers touched a jolt as strong as a lightning strike flashed through her body and her heart burned with the pain of what lay ahead.

Griff strode around to the driver's side of the car, a sudden revelation lightening his mood.

Having extra guests meant more work for Fran—which he didn't like, given the way she was at the moment—but it also meant she'd have more people to attend to on the night and less opportunity to dally with Ian Sinclair if that had been her aim.

He glanced towards her and saw again the paleness he was concerned about, the lack of sparkle in the brown eyes that turned appealingly towards him.

Fran wouldn't betray him with another man. Not after what she'd suffered at Richard's hands. He remembered how her hurt had bothered him, transmitting itself to his body as a physical ache. And a murderous rage towards his unfaithful friend!

The memory made him shudder.

He couldn't be angry with her when she'd already suffered so much.

He touched her shoulder.

'That was almost a fight, wasn't it, Franny?' He spoke softly, wanting to fix things between them, to make everything comfortable again. He wasn't prepared for the tears that welled in her eyes, only to be fiercely blinked away, or for the wrenching pain the sight of those tears caused in his guts.

'It might be better if we fought,' she said, letting him pull her close and resting her head against his shoulder. 'Easier.'

The pain turned to panic. What on earth was this about?

'Are we back to my being too nice?' he demanded. 'Are you bored with our marriage? Do you regret it? Want to get out of it?'

He'd expected an immediate denial, but all he got was her head pressing closer to his neck and her soft lips brushing against his skin. Which made him forget what they were discussing while he kissed her temple, then manoeuvred her into position for a proper, mouth-to-mouth, tongue-tangling kiss.

The first for days, it seemed.

Loud shouts of glee interrupted what was developing in the most promising manner. Fran drew away and fumbled with the long tendrils of hair their embrace had released.

'Trying out the love-bite thing?' Janet asked, as she and Meg continued clapping and yahooing just outside the window.

He waved them away and started the engine, annoyed with himself that he should feel embarrassed about kissing his wife in his own car park.

Wanting more…

Fran told herself it was just a kiss. Like dozens they'd shared. There was nothing wrong with their love life—just with the reason for it and the end results.

She had to be firm, no matter how much it might hurt her. Be practical. It was the least she could do. Wasn't love all about putting the other person's needs first?

'I can squash the party thing—explain to Meg and Janet it's just drinks for a few people because we're having house guests,' she said, hoping to divert Griff's attention from her earlier rash statement—and his mind from any further tempting kisses.

The look Griff shot her told her nothing, but his words killed any hope of reverting to 'the plan'.

'Now I think about it, it's not a bad idea, as long as it's not too much work for you. In fact, why don't we get Patty to cater for it to save you worrying about food? She knows a couple of high school girls who help out with serving at parties and functions—let her handle that side of it.'

'But you don't want a party kind of party,' Fran protested.

To which her infuriating husband replied, 'Oh, I don't know. It might be fun!'

He pulled into the garage at the rear of the house and switched off the engine.

'Now, where were we when we were so rudely interrupted?'

Fran opened the door and fled. She could cope with a party even if it meant amending her plan, she could even cope with Griff's strange attitude towards it. But more seductive kisses?

No way!

She grabbed a pencil and the same notepad she'd not used the previous evening and plonked them down on the divider.

'We were making a list, that's where we were,' she told Griff when he walked in through the back door. 'I'll cook, you write it. Perhaps you could phone people and ask them and just write down the ones who accept.'

'Hey, I thought this was your party,' he protested, but Fran waved his words aside.

'You made it grow,' she reminded him.

He shot her a look that promised the subject was far from settled, but sat down and proceeded to scribble what she assumed were names of invitees.

'You're sure about this?' he asked a few minutes later. 'Once I start making phone calls we can't back out.'

Fran looked up from the potato she was peeling.

'I'd have preferred just the group I'd invited to go with us to the dance,' she said honestly, 'but, given Janet's expectations, I don't see how we can avoid enlarging it.'

The failure of Plan A was weighing heavily on her. Especially as she had no Plan B to take its place. And Griff had looked far from pleased by her reply. In fact, he'd crossed to the phone, grumbling to himself. Something else she'd never seen him do.

She tried to make sense of what was happening, but a heavy tiredness was weighing down her limbs and fogging her brain. Depression over what lay ahead—that's what it was. But the diagnosis failed to make her feel better.

'That's thirty, plus however many you invited to begin with,' Griff announced, coming to sit down to dinner some time later.

He pushed the notebook across the table.

'Here's the list.'

Fran looked at it but didn't read the names, too concerned by the numbers, too desperate to find a Plan B.

'With some people staying here, and friends from out of town, maybe we could have a picnic breakfast on the Sunday morning.'

It was a tentative suggestion, but there was nothing tentative about Griff's reply.

'No!' he said, not only firmly but loudly as well. 'No way! *Niente!* Don't even think about it. It's not on—not happening—'

Fran had to smile as she held up her hands in surrender.

'OK. I get the message. No breakfast, huh?'

'Definitely and unequivocally no breakfast.' He'd simmered down but was still regarding her with suspicion.

'Why this sudden urge to entertain? We've been married nearly twelve months and, apart from having a few friends to dinner occasionally, we've not been into social stuff.'

Uh-oh! Perhaps that was it? As Griff saw an image of his own words in a comic-style balloon in front of his face, he realised what might be behind this entertainment frenzy. Fran was bored with him, bored with the togetherness he found so seductively comfortable—as if being married to her had made his life complete.

That's what she'd meant the other day when she'd said

he was too nice. His mother had hit the nail right on the head. Nice equated with boring!

Afraid his face would betray the turmoil in his mind, he bent over his dinner and consumed it with more speed than manners.

'I want to walk up and see Mum,' he said, when he'd finished the last delicious morsel—and again wondered how Richard could have betrayed a woman who cooked so well and so effortlessly. 'Leave the dishes. I'll do them when I get back.'

'But—'

He stood up and walked around behind her, dropping a kiss on the top of her head. She probably thought he was mad—walking out like this. He hadn't even listened to her reply to his question, his mind too busy assimilating its own answers.

'I don't want her hearing about the party from someone else,' he added. It was a lame excuse but he had to get out of the house—had to think about where all this was leading.

Could Fran be bored enough to leave him? So bored that Ian Sinclair had suddenly become appealing?

Ian Sinclair talked about his prize Angus herd practically non-stop. He talked about weight gains and artificial insemination and prize sperm from imported bulls. What could be more boring than that?

Then there was her sudden about-face over going to Toowoomba for the three-day seminar. First she'd wanted him to go, refusing to acknowledge she was tired and needed a break. In fact, she'd argued he should go.

Now, all at once, she was booked and the matter was settled.

Why? That's what he wanted to know.

Rage hastened his steps so he arrived at his mother's place, high on the hill behind his more modest house, within minutes.

'I'm so glad you came,' she greeted him. 'I wondered if Fran was doing a colour theme for the party. I've some lovely calendulas in the garden right now—bright yellow and orange flowers to a Philistine like you—but if she's chosen pink, there's not much, although the jasmine's out all along the side fence and white goes with anything. The perfume's lovely as well.'

'A colour theme? I come up to tell you we're having a few people in for pre-dinner drinks, and you not only know but you're working on a colour theme? What's wrong with this town? Has everyone gone mad?'

Actually, he'd come up for some maternal comfort—if he could only have worked out some devious way of getting his mother to compare his charms with those of Ian Sinclair's, without revealing his own insecurity.

'I suppose it's because it's Fran's first party we're all excited. It must mean she's really feeling settled now.'

'What do you mean, she's feeling settled now?' he demanded, as his mother's words pounded another blow into his belly. 'She's been here for eighteen months. Of course she's settled. We're married!'

'Yes, dear,' his mother said. 'We all know that, but everyone knew it was a marriage of convenience, and there were a lot of people who had doubts it would work.'

Griff sank down into a chair—mainly because his legs wouldn't hold him upright.

Disbelief turned to anger.

'And who's this everyone you're talking about?' he demanded. 'Do you include yourself? Did you assume it was a marriage of convenience? Did you believe it wouldn't last?'

He glared at his mother in case she hadn't caught on to just how angry he was.

And she had the hide to smile at him.

'I know you better than most.' That was all she'd say,

shifting the conversation with her usual adroitness by asking, 'Do you think the yellow and orange calendulas—or white jasmine? Perhaps you'd better ask Fran.'

He stayed half an hour for politeness' sake, and so his mother couldn't jump to any more erroneous conclusions. She knew him better than most—ha, that was a laugh!

She didn't know he'd married Fran to give her grandchildren, he reminded himself as he stalked down the steps. That he'd put aside his firm commitment to bachelorhood for her sake!

And she had absolutely no idea how he felt about Fran.

Actually, he realised, pausing on the long drive beside a bed of flowers, bleached white by the moonlight so he couldn't recognise them as either calendulas or jasmine, he wasn't entirely certain how he felt about Fran either.

They'd been friends for years, and rescuing her when the divorce had made her so desperately unhappy had seemed a natural thing to do. And marrying her had been a jolly good idea. One of his best, as it had turned out.

As far as he was concerned.

The recurrence of the gut-clenching told him he'd reached the core of the problem. While he might be happy in this marriage—convenient or not—maybe Fran wasn't.

He found himself praying it was just boredom. That a party, a bit more entertaining, would make things right for both of them.

Fran had read his mood swing and knew the casual salute he'd offered had been a bad attempt to disguise the anger she'd somehow caused. And she hadn't even argued about the breakfast!

Now, as she cleaned up the kitchen to avoid thinking about a party she didn't want to have, Griff's behaviour was occupying too much of her mind for it to focus on Plan

B. So when the phone rang she felt nothing but relief, even if it meant a call out to some ill or injured patient.

'Melanie Miller here,' the cool voice announced in response to Fran's hello. 'Would Griff be in?'

'He's not, I'm afraid. Could I help you?' Fran heard the formality in her own voice and wondered why Mrs Miller always affected her this way.

'I'm afraid not. I need to speak to him. Will he be long?'

All night, Fran would have liked to have said, but honesty was always best. 'He's just popped up to see his mother. If it's urgent I could call him there, otherwise I could ask him to phone you when he gets in.'

She hoped the woman couldn't tell she was talking through gritted teeth.

'When he comes in will do. Thank you.'

Ever polite, Mrs Miller—Melanie, as Griff no doubt called her—terminated the conversation, and Fran hung up the receiver. Then, in a gesture worthy of young Peter Drake, she stuck her thumbs in her ears and wiggled her fingers at the phone, sticking her tongue out and pulling a ferocious face at the same time.

'Did someone call you names?'

Griff must have come in while she was talking for he was standing just inside the kitchen where he'd have had a great view of her childish gesture.

Could he also see the tell-tale redness from the heat that burned in her cheeks?

'Just practising,' she said lightly. 'How's Eloise?'

'She wants to know if you're having a colour theme for the party.'

'Colour theme?' Fran faltered.

Until that moment her only concern about the occasion's growth from 'a few drinks' to 'party' was that it had ruined her plan. Now it struck her that this was serious. She was expected to entertain upwards of thirty people and even with Patty from the pie shop doing the catering, she, Fran, would still have a heap of decisions to make, details to organise.

'What do you think?' she asked Griff, aware of desperation in her voice and an added plea in her eyes. 'Should we?'

He hesitated for a moment, then said, 'Why the hell not? Let's go to town with it. Make a splash. Isn't there an old song about "It's my party and I'll do what I want"?'

Fran tried a smile but knew it was a fragile effort. The actual words, she recalled, were 'It's my party, and I'll cry if I want to'. More appropriate than Griff guessed, but she didn't want him to see her crying.

Or suspect it was how she felt!

Searching for a diversion, she remembered the phone call.

'Oh, by the way,' she said, trying for casual this time, 'Mrs Miller phoned. She'd like you to call her back.'

As Griff moved towards the phone Fran wandered into the kitchen to give him privacy.

Not that she wouldn't hear the conversation if she listened.

She ran water in the sink to block any temptation, sprinkled cleanser in and began to rub while she pondered the fact that he'd dialled the number without reference to the phone book.

Colour theme for the party! That's what she should be considering. The dinner-dance was for the firefighters—which brought red to mind. And as it was always held on the third weekend in December, there was a Christmas feel to it. Most of the women guests last year had worn Christmas jewellery of some kind.

Griff came in and touched her on the shoulder.

'I've got to go out. I shouldn't be long.'

She nodded as she would have if it had been any other

patient who'd phoned. The fact that she should be taking calls lay unspoken between them. But her arms ached to hold him to her, and the slow burn of jealousy in the pit of her stomach was a warning of what was to come as she threw women more eligible than Melanie Miller at her husband's head.

Red for Christmas and green for jealousy. Great colour theme for a party!

'Tea and toast your morning order, ma'am?'

Griff's voice roused her from a troubled dream of Christmas elves clad in red and green prodding her with long forks. Perhaps they were small devils, not elves.

'Breakfast in bed?' she said sleepily, struggling into a sitting position while Griff packed extra pillows behind her. She blinked against the brightness of the sun shining through the window. How could she have overslept like this?

'A small indulgence,' her husband said, moving her legs over so he could sit on the edge of the bed. 'I thought I'd let you sleep in.'

Fran glanced towards his side of the bed where the alarm clock was. Only it wasn't.

She looked at Griff.

'I got in late so I took the clock and the phone into the spare room.' He leant forward and slid a hand down her hair. 'Thought you deserved an unbroken night's sleep.'

Fran pressed a hand against her stomach which was squirming uneasily at the thought of Griff coming in late. Griff sleeping in the other room. Griff being so long at Mrs Miller's.

Even if she's at the upper level for childbirth, if he loves her it would be OK, she told herself.

But far from easing her inner turmoil, this thought increased it. Instinct told her Griff wouldn't be happy with

Mrs Miller and, more than anything, she wanted him to be happy.

He deserved to be happy.

'Drink your tea and eat your toast. I've had breakfast so I'll go on down to the surgery and take any early patients, which will give you until nine to put in an appearance.'

Fran nodded. She'd have liked to have asked why he was doing this, but guessed that whatever answer he gave would be an evasion. And she didn't want Griff lying to her.

The most likely explanation was guilt. Guilt over staying out late—over whatever was going on between him and Mrs Miller.

Damn the woman. She *wasn't* right for him.

'Was Mrs Miller ill? Did you have another call after that?'

'No to both,' he said easily, not a bit of guilt showing on his face or lurking in his eyes. 'It's a personal problem with Mrs Miller and much as I wish I could discuss it with you I can't.'

I bet it's personal! Fran thought to herself, determining to come up with a Plan B before the woman had her talons firmly embedded. And possibly a Plan C to distract the older woman from her pursuit.

'But I *have* asked her to the party.'

Fortunately she'd just set the teacup down in its saucer before Griff added this rider, or the bed would have been awash with tea. As it was, the violence of her reaction— her forward lurch—almost unseated Griff from the edge of the bed.

'You've asked Mrs Miller to *my* party?'

He had the cheek to grin at her.

'Oh, it's your party now, is it? Last night it was all my doing! And you said yourself you thought the woman was having trouble making friends. It seemed a natural thing to do.'

Fran couldn't answer, too busy drawing air into her lungs and telling herself that strong hysterics weren't acceptable at this hour of the morning.

'Well, I'll be off,' her infuriating husband added blithely. 'See you later.'

She drank her tea and ate her toast, her mind picturing Griff and Mrs Miller together. Not easy. Griff was such a relaxed person, and Mrs Miller so uptight. In fact, trying to imagine Mrs Miller with her hair mussed from an embrace was so impossible that Fran turned her mind to Plan B.

There *was* no Plan B, and no bright idea illuminated her mind.

With a deep, despairing sigh, she switched to something she could handle. Work. Thinking, she lined up her day's patients. Eloise was coming in at ten, and Jessica Drake, Peter's mother, had a late afternoon appointment.

Which reminded her…

Soothed by routine, and fired by a determination to tie up a few loose ends before leaving town, she found her watch on the bedside table and checked the time.

'I thought I'd go red and green,' she told Eloise in answer to the colour-scheme question. 'I know it seems stupid to have an English Christmas in Australia, but I thought I'd like to do the decorations with traditional wreaths and garlands of plaited evergreens and ivy around the windows. Relying on your garden, of course.'

'I've holly as well, but there are no berries on it at this time of the year, although my Bangalow palm has red berries on it at the moment. We could cheat.'

Fran smiled at her mother-in-law.

'I'm so pleased to hear that ''we'',' she said. 'I wasn't

sure where to begin. But you're to supervise only,' she warned. 'No overdoing it.'

'I won't,' Eloise promised. 'I've learned to live with this stupid heart of mine.'

'Which reminds me, you're here for an appointment, not to discuss the party.'

She helped Eloise onto the examination couch, wanting to check her lungs, to listen for the bubbling or crackling noise that indicated secretions in the tiny bronchioles.

'I saw a programme on TV about patients with congestive heart failure on long-term digoxin therapy being taken off it and the majority not showing any ill effects.'

Fran threw her hands into the air.

'Now everyone's an expert!' she said. 'If it's not a magazine article, it's a TV programme or, would you believe, something they found on the internet? And what exactly did the experiment hope to achieve?'

Her hands moved as she spoke, feeling for the signs that veins were under pressure from a malfunctioning ventricle.

'According to the doctor on the show, a lot of people keep taking it, and doctors prescribing it, although it isn't needed once whatever caused the episode of heart failure is cured.'

Fran considered this.

'Perhaps that's valid in cases where the heart problem was a one-off thing, but in your case we're dealing with damage cause by a viral infection when you were a child. We're using the digoxin—and not a lot of it when you consider you're only on a minimum maintenance dose of 25 mg—to keep your heart stimulated enough to do its job.'

'So you wouldn't recommend me going off it, even with you and Griff fussing over me the way you do in case things went wrong.'

Fran helped Eloise to a sitting position and wrapped a blood-pressure cuff around her upper arm.

'What could go wrong would be you going into heart failure, and I'd prefer you didn't do that for at least the next few weeks. In fact, make that a month and get us through New Year as well.'

She was teasing, but in her heart she hoped Eloise's health would remain stable for at least a year. That should be enough time for Griff to court his new wife quickly, and for the chosen woman to produce a baby for Eloise to hold in her arms.

'No trial before Christmas?' Eloise said, as Fran released the air slowly from the cuff, listening for the missing beats in the systolic pressure.

'No trial, full stop, as far as I'm concerned,' she told Eloise. 'But if you want to talk it over with Griff in the New Year, and he agrees to monitor it, and you, on a daily basis…'

She stopped, fussing with the instrument, writing down a note on Eloise's card, hoping she looked professionally distracted, not startled that she'd so nearly revealed her intention to extricate herself not only from her marriage but from Summerfield as well.

'We'll see,' Eloise said. 'Are you doing your vampire thing this visit?'

Fran smiled at the older woman, although the pain in her heart reminded her that Griff wasn't all she'd lose when she left Summerfield.

'No, we did full blood tests last time, remember,' she said gently. 'And an ECG, which would show up any serious imbalance in your potassium levels. If you continue to be sensible, you should sail through the Christmas festivities in fine fettle.'

She hesitated, then remembered how the party idea had come about and added, 'I know you don't want to go to the dinner-dance, but would you like to join us for the party? Griff could pick you up, and we could drop you home on our way to the hall.'

Eloise shook her head.

'Parties never appealed to me. When Griff's father was alive, I went to all the social occasions in town because people expected the doctor and his wife to attend, but most of the time I'd rather have been at home with a good book.'

'Now, that I can relate to,' Fran told her, remembering how much she'd hated the partying Richard had liked to do. Was that why he'd sought diversions elsewhere? Had she been at fault in not keeping up with him?

'I know what you're thinking, and you're wrong,' Eloise said to her. 'No one could keep up with Richard.'

Had she been frowning that Eloise had picked upon her thoughts?

'Richard comes across as totally committed—to work, to friends, to whatever he's got his mind set on at the time,' Eloise continued. 'But when the boys first met at boarding school and Richard started coming to us for his holidays, I soon learned he lacked staying power. He had a short attention span. Almost impossible to keep occupied. He'd start something then get bored with it and be hanging around my feet, asking what he could do next. He was the same with friends—first one and then another. Griff was the only constant in his life.'

'Then why get married?' Fran said, asking aloud the question she'd asked herself a thousand times.

Eloise didn't answer. She stood up and straightened her clothes, then picked up her handbag.

'Barney will be waiting to drive me home,' she said, moving towards the door when normally she'd have sat awhile and talked. She put her hand on the knob then turned back towards Fran. 'Richard always wanted to have what Griff had,' she said softly. 'For a time, he seduced me into loving him almost as much as I loved Griff, then I realised he wanted me to love him more and I began to feel sorry for him.'

Fran was so puzzled by the cryptic remark that she once again failed to walk to the reception area with her patient—instead, standing and staring at the open door as she tried to work out if Eloise was simply making conversation or telling her something important.

But no matter how she turned the words about in her head, she couldn't find any connection between her marriage to Richard and Griff's relationship with his mother.

CHAPTER FIVE

'MEG said the milk will fortify you for the rush and the biscuits are for carbohydrates.' Susie interrupted her thoughts, pushing through the door with a tray in her hand. 'She said can you eat and consult as Griff's been called out to an accident and she'd like to alternate the patients until he returns.'

Fran nodded her agreement. Alternating—taking one of Griff's patients then one of her own—was their normal practice when one or other of them was called out during working hours. In theory, it meant no one should be kept waiting too long.

In practice, it meant everyone had to wait.

'Just make sure I've got the files,' she warned Susie, and took a gulp of milk—not her favourite drink—and a bite of biscuit.

Hank Benson, the local baker, was the first of Griff's patients.

'If I wasn't in so much damn pain I'd have waited for him to come back,' Hank told her. 'It's my waterworks and damn embarrassing it is, discussing such things with a woman.'

Fran put on a suitably concerned expression.

'What's the problem?' she asked.

'Apart from having to go every five minutes?' Hank muttered at her. 'It hurts like bloody hell, that's the problem. Burns like billy-o! Bloody awful it is, and, no, it doesn't look any different from the way it always does and I'm not pulling it out for you to look at.'

'The most likely thing is cystitis. That's a lower urinary

85

tract infection either in the ureters, the tubes leading down from your kidneys, or in the bladder itself. There's another possibility, an upper tract infection, pyelonephritis, which can also attack the kidneys.'

'Does it matter which I have?' Hank asked, and Fran smiled at him.

'Not in the slightest at this stage,' she said, checking through his file for any mention of recurrent kidney problems or suspected kidney disease.

'As you're apparently as healthy as a horse, I'll give you a shot of kanamysin which should fix you up almost immediately. If you get a recurrence within two weeks, it would point to pyelonephritis and we can run further tests.'

'Give me a shot?' Hank moaned.

'Why not?' Fran said, in her most heartless voice. 'Don't be a baby.'

She picked up the phone and told Janet what she wanted, then turned back to her patient.

'And while we're talking shots, I hope to see you next week when we're doing diphtheria boosters at the council chambers. Tell your mates—see if you can get the men of Summerfield to show the way!'

Hank looked at her as if she were mad.

'Booster shots are for kids,' he complained.

'And how many grown-ups went to hospital last year with diphtheria?' Fran demanded.

'They were old people,' Hank reminded her.

'Like you will be one day,' Fran said. 'If you don't get diphtheria in the meantime.'

He was grumbling to himself about bossy women when Janet came in and set down a kidney dish holding swabs, a disposable syringe and needle and a vial of the drug.

'Want me to hold him down while you jab?' she asked Fran.

'Ha!' Fran said, grinning at her patient as she drew up

.5 of a gram into the syringe. 'So your reputation goes ahead of you. You've always been a wimp!'

'I am not,' Hank protested, but as Fran swabbed his meaty biceps, he turned pale and shuddered.

'It won't hurt much,' she said, more gently now she'd realised he was seriously upset. 'I'll be as quick as I can.'

She slid the tip of the needle beneath the skin and injected the fluid into his muscle.

'Here, hold this,' she told him, pressing a cotton-wool ball on the site.

'You've finished? You're done?'

Fran patted the top of his balding head.

'All done,' she affirmed. 'But sit still for a minute. I wouldn't like you passing out when you stand up. There's too much of you to get upright again.'

She put a strip of transparent tape over the cotton ball, then walked around her desk to write up her notes.

'I want you drinking a lot of water—as much as you can manage—for the next few days, then six to eight glasses a day after that.'

'Does beer count?' he asked. 'I can manage six to eight glasses of that and I'll tell Marg you told me to drink it.'

'Beer doesn't count,' Fran told him firmly. 'Water. It's good for you.'

Hank shuddered, but Fran guessed the infection had caused sufficient pain for him to take her advice. For a while, at least.

'You want any special order for your party?' he asked, and Fran gave an inward shudder. She knew news spread like wildfire in small communities, but this was ridiculous.

'Better let me know as soon as you can as I'm doing the sweets for the dinner dance—profiteroles—so I'll be busy.' Hank stood up as he added this caution.

'I'm asking Patty to cater. I'll tell her to talk to you,' Fran replied, as she, too, rose to her feet, ready to accompany him out. 'But in the meantime, drink lots of water, and come back to see me or Griff if it recurs.'

'I'll probably see Griff,' Hank said. 'But you're not so bad for a woman.'

Fran smiled, aware she'd been paid a rare compliment by one of the die-hard Griff-supporters. Then her smile faded as she realised it no longer mattered. Although maybe her replacement in the surgery, if it was a woman, would benefit from the ground she'd gained among the locals.

'Jenny, would you like to come through?'

Fran checked the waiting room as she waited for Jenny. Not too bad at the moment. Mrs Miller was there—presumably Griff's next patient. Had she been told Griff wasn't available?

For a moment, Fran considered asking Meg, but as she hated any kind of whispered conversation carried on in front of patients she let it slide.

'How are you feeling?' she asked Jenny as the pregnant woman made herself at home, stripping down to bra and panties and climbing onto the examination couch.

'Not so bad now I'm lying down.'

'And not so good either by the sound of that reply.' Fran spoke gently, her eyes taking in the slight swelling around Jenny's ankles. 'Did you give Janet a urine sample?'

Jenny nodded. 'She also weighed me and did my blood pressure because she knew you were running late. And before you ask, my blood pressure is fine but I've put on a couple of extra kilos. Janet's already scolded me about that.'

Fran studied her patient, seeking any signs of oedema in her wrists or around her eyes.

Jenny looked tired, but why wouldn't she? With a three-year-old and eighteen-month-old twins running around the house. After the twins, she and her husband, Greg, had decided their family had been complete. This pregnancy had been an accident and, although they'd opted to go through with it, Jenny was finding it hard.

'What's the worst part at the moment?' Fran asked.

'Not getting enough sleep,' Jenny said promptly. 'I could probably doze off right here and now. It's bad enough not having time to rest during the day because the wretches don't ever synchronise their daytime sleeps, but the nights are dreadful. Greg gets up to the twins if they cry in the night, which they invariably do, but I wake up anyway and then find it hard to get back to sleep.'

She paused, then smiled ruefully at Fran.

'I can't seem to get comfortable. Everything aches more at night. Even my legs, which should feel better when they're not carting me around. And then there are the cramps. I've tried every old wives' tale from corks in the bed to salt tablets.'

'No salt tablets,' Fran said firmly as she felt Jenny's abdomen, checking the position of the foetus, listening to its heartbeat. 'Your kidneys have to work harder when you're pregnant, so look after them—don't overload them.'

She checked the fundal height measurement, working through the now weekly routine.

'I only took them for a couple of days, and they didn't make any difference,' Jenny admitted, as Fran's examination moved on to the bulging veins on Jenny's legs. She could feel the ache in them herself.

'Have support stockings helped?' she asked. 'Resting with your legs up, propped against a wall?'

Jenny nodded.

'The stockings help when I remember to put them on.' She grinned again. 'I know that sounds pathetic but, honestly, most days it could be ten o'clock before I realise I'm still in my nightdress.'

Remembering the trim, fit, efficient young woman she'd

monitored during the last stages of Jenny's previous pregnancy, Fran found this hard to believe.

And must have shown her surprise for Jenny explained.

'Here's how it goes. Almost without fail, as the sun breaks over the hills one of the kids lets out a wail. Because I know Greg's been up during the night, and also because I don't want whichever child it is waking the other two, I leap out of bed and grab the wailer.'

'That makes sense, even if the early morning thing makes my blood run cold,' Fran said. 'What happens next?'

'Next I change the child—I now keep spare clothes in the living room so the house always looks a mess—then we both sit like zombies in front of the television and watch the early morning aerobics session. That's the extent of my exercise these days.'

'Why early morning aerobics?'

Jenny chuckled.

'It's all that's on—or perhaps there are other shows, but all the kids are mesmerised by the action so I have a chance to doze off again, with the child on my knee. By the time that finishes, another is usually awake, and the first one has remembered he—it's invariably one of the twins—woke up because he was hungry, and he starts demanding breakfast, and so it goes. Next thing I know it's ten o'clock, Greg's gone to work and I'm still in my night attire.'

'That's understandable,' Fran said, but her mind was working on how she could engineer a possible break for Jenny.

'I know your family is in Brisbane, but what about Greg's parents? Could they help?'

'They do what they can, but they're dairy farmers and have cows to milk twice a day. Lorelle stays with them quite often. She's developing more and more 'girl' traits and hates getting her shoes dirty so she's content to sit on the fence and watch the proceedings. But having the twins racing around the dairy between the cows' legs is too much to even consider.'

'Can you sleep during the day?' Fran asked. 'I mean, would you be able to if Greg's mother had Lorelle and someone looked after the twins for a few hours?'

'Could I sleep?' Jenny said. 'I'd sell my soul for a few free hours. Sleeping would be easy. Even resting with my feet up and cat-napping would probably help.'

'Well, I'll volunteer for Saturday,' Fran told her. 'Griff's on call so I'll be free. If it doesn't suit your mother-in-law to have Lorelle, then I could take all three. We can go to the park, then home for lunch, and they can have a play in Mrs Griffiths's garden after lunch. I'd offer to have them overnight, but as they don't know me very well it might be too much for them.'

As she made the offer, and saw tears glimmer in Jenny's eyes, she realised it was another local need. Some form of support for mothers of young families. Perhaps honorary grandparents who could take small children for a walk occasionally to give the mother a break.

'I can't let you do that,' Jenny protested.

'Of course you can. Just make sure you have a proper rest. No using the time to tidy the house.'

Jenny sat up, then swung her legs over the side of the table and felt for the footstool.

'May I do a quick dash through the supermarket to stock up on a few essentials?' she asked. 'Try shopping with three toddlers if you really want to know what hell is like.'

Shopping with one toddler would have been nice, Fran thought as the emotion she was determined to keep at bay sneaked up on her.

'I'll concede the shopping,' she promised, steadying Jenny as she stood up, then pulling the curtain to give her privacy while she dressed. 'As long as you include a sleep in there some time.'

She wrote up her notes then walked with Jenny back to the reception room.

'Mrs Miller has said she'll wait for Griff, so could you take Mrs Stevens next, then, if Griff's not back, Mr Walsh? We're going well and should catch up during the lunch-break.'

'Providing you're not wanting lunch yourself.' Janet came up behind her to add this waiver. 'I've dressed Mr Walsh's leg but he needs a repeat on his antibiotics. I could have phoned the chemist and told them we'd drop the script in later, but I think he's looking forward to the novelty of seeing you instead of Griff.'

Fran was pleased some of the older male patients were now accepting her, but knowledge that it had all come too late more than outweighed her pleasure. She called to Mrs Stevens and walked with her back to her room.

'There's nothing wrong with me,' Mrs Stevens began. 'It's Albert.'

Fran forgot her gloom, closed her eyes, and prayed Albert wasn't an animal.

'He's my cousin and he's not quite right, if you know what I mean, and he's always lived at home with Aunt May but she's getting on and she can't be doing all she did before, besides, when I think about it, it's not much of a life for Albert either.'

Processing this information took a few seconds, but Fran agreed with the sentiment.

'I know the government provides support for people who can't live alone,' she told Mrs Stevens, 'and in some cases, they will help with accommodation. Albert would have to be assessed by a professional team so they could work out what his needs are, and then take it from there.'

She tried to think if she'd ever seen anyone in town who might possibly be Albert.

'I could give you the name of a health worker to contact,

but perhaps you should make sure this is what your aunt wants.'

'I don't think it's what Aunt May wants at all,' Mrs Stevens said crossly. 'Aunt May thinks she's managing just fine, but she forgets it's me who does her shopping every week, and me who drives it out to her place and usually does some washing or a bit of housework, cleaning the kitchen and bathroom mainly, while I'm out there.'

With a quick glance downward at the file to check Mrs Stevens's date of birth, and an even quicker calculation, Fran worked out her patient was seventy-two. A very active seventy-two, but still…

'How long have you been doing this?' she asked Mrs Stevens. 'And how old is your aunt?'

Mrs Stevens used her fingers for her calculations.

'My mother died eight years ago, and she was sick before that. I started when she was ill and couldn't go herself. Aunt May turned ninety this year.'

Fran closed her eyes to hide her reaction. Life in the country never failed to amaze her, although she guessed this could have happened in the city.

'So you've been keeping an eye on her for close to ten years,' Fran worked out. 'Was she ill or frail before that? Why was your mother looking after her?'

'Someone had to,' Mrs Stevens announced. 'There was Albert to consider, not just Aunt May. When Uncle Fred died my mother tried to persuade May to sell the farm and come and live in town but she refused. Said it was Albert's heritage. Some heritage, with the place so run-down and overgrown you can't hardly get up the drive.'

'And what does Albert do all day?' Fran asked.

'He chops the wood, looks after the garden, feeds the chickens and collects the eggs. He can cook simple things like porridge and vegetables, and he likes making cakes.'

Fran was fascinated at this insight into other people's

lives but not certain there was anything she could do. Except, perhaps, to ease the burden on Mrs Stevens.

'How far out of town is this farm? Would meals-on-wheels deliver there if they were contacted?'

'Aunt May won't have them,' Mrs Stevens said. 'I suggested that once, and told her about the home help she could have. It's because of Albert. She doesn't want strangers staring at him. At least, that's what I suppose she thinks. I don't think she ever once brought him to town, even when he was a baby. Until Uncle Fred died he did all the shopping.'

'Short of Albert having two heads, I can't imagine people staring at him,' Fran said. 'The community these days is far more accepting of people who are a little different.'

'He's only got one head,' Mrs Stevens assured her. 'Though from the way Aunt May carries on, refusing to even think about moving, you'd wonder.'

It was hard to imagine a ninety-year-old woman still wielding such power. She must have a will of iron, Fran thought, while her brain teased at some way to solve Mrs Stevens's dilemma.

'How's your arthritis?' she asked, and Mrs Stevens held up her hands to display the knobbly joints.

'Perhaps if you explained to your aunt that the housework is too painful for you now. Tell her again about home help, and explain that you get help yourself—'

Mrs Stevens was shaking her head, but at the same time looked hopefully at Fran.

Light dawned. It explained the appointment.

'You'd like me to contact her and tell her you're not well?' she said weakly as the thought of confronting this formidable old woman made her feel faint.

'She'd have to believe it, then,' Mrs Stevens told Fran. 'I brought her phone number.'

She slid a piece of paper across the desk. 'And I've

talked to Lucy Crane who runs the home-help office, and she says whoever she sends out will take the groceries. I'll still visit, but perhaps not every week. After all, if Aunt May wants company she could move to town.'

Fran hid a smile. It had taken ten years for Mrs Stevens to revolt against this regime, but now she'd decided to stand firm she was going the whole way.

'I'll phone you when I've spoken to her,' Fran promised, and saw a shadow of disappointment flash across Mrs Stevens's face.

'I'm sorry, but I can't attend to it right now. Griff's been called out to an accident up in the hills. I'm taking double patients,' she said by way of explanation, although in truth she wanted to talk to him about this first. There was a very fine line between doing what you could to help a patient, and intruding into other people's lives.

Mrs Stevens nodded and rose to her feet.

'I won't keep doing it no matter what she says!' she muttered, and Fran guessed familial guilt was already weakening her resolve.

'We'll work something out,' she promised. 'Even if we have to do it gradually. Maybe for a start you could go with the home-help worker—show her what your routine is, and reassure your aunt while the worker is there.'

Mrs Stevens nodded.

'That's a good idea.'

She let Fran steer her back to the reception area.

'Griff's back,' Meg said, at the same moment Fran realised that Mrs Miller was no longer in the waiting room.

'Could you tell him I need a few minutes of his time if he breaks for lunch later?' Fran replied. They often communicated through Meg, who was more likely to see them between patients, but because of all that lay between them at the moment Fran felt the distancing effect of such a message.

And regretted it.

She saw another three patients before Meg announced she'd caught up.

'I told Griff you were nearly done. He's fixing a sandwich and will bring it through to you.'

Fran wandered back into her room, kicked off her shoes, pulled out the middle drawer of her desk and rested her feet on it. She guessed it was the bottled-up emotion, the strain of knowing she had to go, that made her feel so tired. After all, she'd had a good night's sleep—apart from the dream.

But when Griff came in, tray in hand, one glance at his face made her forget her own tiredness.

'Put it down! Sit! You've got to stop waiting on me. Start looking after yourself.' She stood up and came around the desk, waving him into a chair then standing behind him, her hands on his shoulders, her fingers already massaging into the knotted muscles at the base of his neck.

He moved his head, as if trying to click the kinks out of his spine, and gave in to her ministrations, but the tension was hard to shift.

'Bad accident?' she asked, digging her fingers in hard in an effort to make things better for him.

'A timber-cutter up in the hills. It's so mechanised these days, you wonder how accidents happen. In this case a log rolled on him, trapping him by the legs. We called the helicopter rescue service and medivaced him straight to Brisbane.'

Minor injuries went to town or, if in need of specialist treatment, to Toowoomba. Flying him direct to the state capital meant he was very bad.

'And even then he'll probably lose both his legs.'

'But not his life,' Fran reminded her usually upbeat husband.

'Isn't it?' Griff asked, reaching up to clasp one of her

ministering hands in a firm grip. 'Will he thank us for that when he comes back to the reality of life without the only job he's ever known? To keeping his wife and family on an invalid pension?'

Fran changed from massaging to caressing, moving her fingers up so she could knead his scalp, as if the movement might chase away his gloomy thoughts.

'Hey,' she reminded him, 'you're the optimist in this partnership. You said yourself timber-cutting is largely mechanical these days—perhaps he can get hand controls on one of the machines. Or be a foreman. And remember, most of those men are woodsmen through and through. They carve bits of it for fun. They whittle it. There'll be plenty he can do.'

Griff chuckled.

'Talk about a dose of my own medicine.' He shifted and pulled her down on his knee. 'Thank you, Madam Wife!'

But his kiss said more than thank you. If Fran hadn't known better and been so determined to set him free, she might have let herself believe it said I love you.

'The tea's getting cold,' he murmured against her throat. 'And if we go much further I won't be able to stop and someone is sure to walk in.'

'Coward,' Fran teased. 'I bet it's because I'm getting too heavy on your knee, and not fear of discovery.'

She walked back around to her chair so the desk provided a safety barrier between them, and the distance, though not great, would hide the sadness she knew would be reflected in her eyes.

'So, now I've told you my problem, what's yours?' Griff asked, as they both, aware of time restraints, tackled the sandwiches he'd made.

'Two-headed Albert!' Fran said, and smiled at Griff's reaction. 'Actually, Mrs Stevens assures me he hasn't got two heads and it's mean-spirited of me to get a rise that way, but do you know this Albert? Or an old lady called May who lives out of town?'

'I thought I knew—or knew of—everyone, but May and Albert? It's not ringing any bells. If they're locals Mum would probably know them. What's the problem?'

Fran recounted the tale Mrs Stevens had told her.

'Poor woman. I can't believe it's gone on so long and no one's done anything about it.'

'I don't think Mrs Stevens has minded helping out,' Fran explained, 'until recently, when I guess she's feeling a bit tired of it all, and restricted by the regular Friday duty.'

Griff took another sandwich.

'I wasn't thinking of Mrs Stevens, but of her aunt,' he said. 'Bearing a child who was considered different, then wanting to protect him as best she could. When you consider the counselling available today—the services and schooling for children with special needs—I wonder how long ago it was. How old Albert is.'

'I didn't ask,' Fran told him. 'But, no matter how old he is, if his mother has protected him all this time, it will be hard to change her attitude now. And perhaps not in Albert's best interests to suddenly thrust him into any other life.'

Griff grinned at her.

'I wasn't going to advocate rushing into things,' he said. 'In fact, I'm glad it's your problem, not mine. I'm really not sure where I'd start. A phone call doesn't seem quite the way to go.'

Fran nodded.

'I'd begun to realise that,' she said. 'Phoning a total stranger isn't good at the best of times, but to phone a ninety-year-old for the express purpose of disrupting her life would be unnecessarily harsh, now I've considered it.'

She ate another sandwich, thinking that food might help the tiredness.

'I'll talk to your mother first. She might have some knowledge of the woman, some idea of how best to approach her. Then maybe I could phone and ask if I could visit. It would be better to see the situation first hand, and also be there when I explain about Mrs Stevens.'

She doodled on her scrap paper, while her mind played out possible scenarios, so at first she didn't notice Griff's silence. And when it was noticeable enough for her to look at him, she found him studying her—too intently for comfort.

'Smut on my nose? Love-bite?' She repeated the words Janet had used. 'No, I know I haven't one of those.'

'Don't we both,' he said heavily, then he shook his head and smiled again—reverting to the Griff she knew. 'You don't have to take on all these outside problems,' he said gently. 'Now you've settled in, learn to pace yourself. Prioritise. Work out what other people can do, rather than personally rushing to the rescue every time.'

'Well,' Fran snorted, partly to hide the pain his 'settled in' had caused, 'that's great advice, coming from you! Did you have to give yourself more work by organising the immunisation drive? And what about the Rotary Club's Gardening Frenzy? Don't you always arrange to have that weekend off duty so you can join in the onslaught on the older people's lawns and gardens? Talk about pots calling kettles black. If I get involved, it's only because that's how I thought we worked, what country practice was all about.'

His smile made her bones melt.

'And so it is, my Franny,' he said softly. 'I just don't want you overdoing it. Is it wrong for me to feel protective of you?'

Yes! she wanted to shout. I don't want you to feel anything towards me.

Well, love would have been nice if things had worked out better, but given the circumstances—

'Where do you go?' he asked.

'Go?' Fran repeated.

'When your eyes darken and the lights go out in them as if you've closed the door on your thoughts. Shut me out. I feel it's happening more often lately, Fran, and wondered if it's something you'd like to talk about. We're friends as well as lovers, remember. We've always been friends.'

Fran's heart ached at the gentleness in his voice, at all she would lose, for their friendship would never survive her defection.

'I was thinking of something else, that's all,' she said, masking the lie with lightness. Then a random synapse in her mind provided the perfect excuse. 'Actually, of what you'd say about me getting too involved when I told you I've promised to mind the Smith twins on Saturday.'

'You've done what?' her husband roared.

It was becoming a habit, this roaring thing!

'It's only for a few hours. Jenny's desperately tired. I can't think why there isn't something organised by one of the church or service groups to provide occasional care for children when their mothers need a break.'

'You've enough projects on the go already,' Griff said, the sternness in his voice warning Fran to drop the subject.

Fortunately, before he could get back onto the previous one, Meg tapped on the door to warn them the afternoon patients were arriving.

'I'll see you later.' Her husband made it more a challenge than a promise but, with luck, by evening, after a visit to Eloise, she'd know enough about Aunt May and Albert and could use them to provide a diversion.

Not that there was anything Griff could say that she wasn't already telling herself. She had to get less involved in this town, not more.

Leaving would be hard enough, but if she was caught up in a multitude of projects, it would be impossible.

No, not impossible.

CHAPTER SIX

'MAY TURNER. Her husband, Fred, ran beef cattle. Not stud cattle if I remember, more dealing. Buying cows in calf and selling off the calves when they were about half-grown. I suppose if Summerfield had an aristocracy, Fred Turner considered himself it.'

Eloise frowned out at her garden. She and Fran were sitting on her front verandah and she was obviously searching her memory for more information on the Turners.

'Something happened. I remember my Griff talking about it, but I think it was before his time as well. I haven't heard anything of the family for years. I used to see Fred when he was alive. Came in every Friday to the sales then you'd see him around the town. I suppose I assumed she was dead. You say there's a son?'

'Who has been hidden away all his life if Mrs Stevens is to be believed.' Fran, too, looked out over the garden, where bright red gerberas had caught her eye and started another train of thought.

Had her mind always been so easily distracted? Or was it the thought of what lay ahead that made it skip from one idea to another like an erratic bee in a garden full of flowers?

'Well, I've never known of a child or seen him, child or man!' Eloise announced. She gave the garden more consideration then added, 'You'll need to tread carefully, Fran. It's a delicate situation.'

'But it will be even more delicate if something happens to Mrs Turner and Albert is left with no one familiar in his life. Apart from Mrs Stevens, who isn't too happy about her role.'

'Family ties are important,' Eloise said, 'but remember not to let them strangle you. Duty can wear many faces and some of them might be false.'

Bemused by the conversational switch—if it was a switch—Fran turned to face her mother-in-law, who was continuing to study her garden with a bland look concealing whatever might lie behind her cryptic words.

'The gerberas will fit your red and green, with some foliage from the cypress out the back or perhaps the pencil pines. And I've those two nice bay trees in pots at the bottom of the steps. I thought if we put red bows and perhaps a little baby's breath in among the leaves…'

Fran looked down to where the two trees stood guard at the edge of the driveway, their round tops like dark green balls. They *would* look good with red bows and some sprays of gypsophila…

Maybe her thoughts were erratic because there was so much to plan between now and Christmas. So much to do.

'You should write a list.' Eloise's voice startled her, but the advice was excellent. With a list she could tick off each job as it was done. At the top she'd put, 'Work out Plan B.'

'And I'll tell Barney what to keep. He tends to trim things back when he has a spare moment, and we don't want him trimming things you might need.'

Fran realised Eloise meant a list of flowers she'd want, and hastened to get with it.

'I'm minding Jenny Smith's twins on Saturday,' she said. 'If it's all right with you, I thought I might bring them up here for an hour or so. I can look at the garden then and work out what would look good.'

Eloise agreed, and they chatted amiably for a while until Fran felt she should get moving. She said goodbye and set

off down towards her house. There was a meal to prepare—
Griff had already done breakfast and lunch—and lists to
write.

And Plan B to hatch.

Her lungs contracted and her heart beat faster, even
thinking about handing him over to another woman, but
Griff had saved her sanity when Richard had deserted her—
now it was her turn to do something for him.

'Your mother knows of Mrs Stevens's Aunt May
Turner.' Griff was standing in the kitchen, peeling a carrot,
when Fran returned, and she introduced the topic in the
hope it might divert his mind from other matters. 'And I'm
doing dinner. You've done all the meals today.'

She took the carrot and the peeler from him, which
wasn't such a good idea as it left his hands free to wrap
around her waist. The warmth of his body pressed against
her back—too familiar, too seductive.

'We could have a late dinner,' he whispered in her ear,
and Fran had to summon all her will-power—and an image
of Mrs Miller sitting in the waiting room—to resist the
unspoken suggestion.

'But Eloise doesn't know of Albert,' she managed to say,
pretending to be deaf to his suggestion and totally unaf-
fected by his caresses. Not easy when he must surely feel
the nerves jumping under her skin!

'Considering they wouldn't have known there was anything wrong with him before his birth, you'd assume his
mother saw a doctor, so perhaps…'

'You're not suggesting we go through those boxes of
files down in the surgery basement in search of your
Albert.' Griff sounded horrified—so much so that he
stopped nuzzling her neck to straighten up and give the
words some force. 'Anyway, what's the point? You know
he exists.'

Fran nodded.

'You're right. There is no point. Perhaps I could use the immunisation programme as an excuse—phone Mrs Turner and suggest that if she can't come to us I could go to her.'

Griff chuckled and released her, crossing to the refrigerator and taking out a bottle of soda water.

'That should go down well,' he said. 'Considering they never see anyone but Mrs Stevens, they're hardly likely to pick up germs.'

'Albert chops the wood,' Fran told him huffily, although she agreed the idea wasn't one hundred per cent foolproof. 'And on a farm there could be tetanus.'

'Tetanus is good,' Griff teased, pouring a lime and soda and setting it on the bench in front of her. 'Yes, she might go for tetanus! Now, having sorted that one out, what about the Smith twins? And I made a list of people who might help out with Peter Drake. Are you still working on that project?'

Fran swallowed a huge sigh. It was one thing acknowledging to herself that things were getting on top of her, quite another to admit it to her infuriatingly insightful husband.

'Yes, of course. Actually, his mother was in to see me this afternoon. She's suffering aches and pains in her joints and wondered if it could be from standing up all day at the pharmacy. Is Jessica local? Do you know her parents? Is there a family history of arthritis? I did ask her that question, but she was very vague about it.'

Griff didn't answer, and Fran, after pulling a carton of eggs from the refrigerator, continued, 'She mentioned Peter. Apparently she's aware the teachers consider him a gifted child and she's saving up for a computer for him to have at home. Life must be hard for a single mother.'

'Jessica's a good kid,' Griff said, and Fran, who, since the attractive, dark-haired Jessica's visit, had been wondering how Griff would feel about a ready-made family, didn't know whether to feel pleased or disappointed at his perception of the young woman. A kid? 'And I'm glad she's coming to the party with the crowd from the pharmacy. It will do her good to get out a bit and socialise.'

His obvious lack of interest convinced Fran to cross Jessica off her list of candidates. And speaking of lists—wasn't that where this conversation had started?

Lists and plans—she was going bananas, trying to keep track!

'Thanks for the list of possible helpers. I'll start phoning people tomorrow.'

'And the Smith twins?' Griff persisted.

Fran abandoned the eggs she was now beating for a frittata and turned to face him.

'Jenny's desperately tired. I couldn't think of anything else to do to help her out.'

Griff stepped closer and pulled the pins from her hair, letting it tumble around her shoulders then pushing it back from her face and tucking strands behind her ears.

'You're tired yourself, Franny,' he said, his voice husky with concern. 'You need to do less, not more.'

He leaned forward and kissed her gently on the lips.

She knew what lay behind his words. She'd used tiredness as an excuse to avoid intimacy between them over the past week, hoping the lack of closeness might make her departure easier. But her body ached for the solace only Griff's could give it, and the pain in her heart made her wonder if she was mad to consider leaving him.

It's for him you're doing it, she reminded herself, and she turned away, seized the bowl of half-melded eggs and continued beating.

'A couple of good nights' sleep, that's all I need,' she said, hoping she sounded more convincing than she felt.

'Is it now?' he said, accepting her rejection, his voice

cooler than her drink. 'I've some work to do on the articles for the paper. I'll be in the study.'

It was the way things had to be, Fran told herself. She finished fixing their meal, called Griff to eat and over dinner chatted determinedly about work.

Not fooling around with Griff after dinner, not sitting pressed close against him and laughing at the inanities of some television compere, it meant she had more time to tie up some of the loose ends fluttering around her like the torn streamers after a party.

A metaphor for this time of her life if ever she'd heard one!

'I've three helpers each willing to give one morning a week to Peter,' she announced the following evening. Having avoided her husband all day, keeping busy on the phone in her gaps between patients, there was plenty to relay over dinner. 'I gave the names and phone numbers to Jackie, who's thrilled.'

'I bet she is,' Griff said, with enough bite in his voice to show Fran he could see through this ploy of cheerful work-related prattle but would go along with it for now.

'And I spoke to Mrs Stevens's Aunt May and I've asked Meg to keep a couple of hours free of appointments on Friday morning so I can go out and visit her while Mrs Stevens is there. I told Mrs Turner I was fairly new to the district and wanted to meet everyone so I'd know who was who. I don't think she quite understood who I was or what I wanted, but I bulldozed over her half-hearted objections.'

Fran felt the faint heat of embarrassment beneath her skin and hoped it wasn't showing. She hated deceit of any kind, but knew she'd been less than honest in her approach to the old woman.

And the only idea she had for Plan B involved even more devious manoeuvring.

Griff saw the sheen of pink colouring his wife's skin,

and wondered why a visit to a strange old woman should produce such a reaction. And how they'd reached the point where they sat across the table from each other like polite strangers.

Not that he intended making the first move this time. Not when Fran had made it quite clear his caresses were no longer welcome.

She could come to him.

Beg for the loving he was certain she'd enjoyed as much as he had!

Actually, the begging could be fun…

'I'll walk up after dinner and see Mum,' he said, dragging his wilful mind off erotic fancies to focus on the problem at hand. If this Mrs Turner lived out along the same road as Ian Sinclair's property—

What could he do?

Forbid her to go?

He must have sighed, for suddenly she was Fran again. His friend, if not his lover. She reached across and touched his hand.

'Are you OK? I've been going on and on about my day, and haven't asked about yours. Is it the timber-cutter you're concerned over? Did you phone the hospital?'

He realised he hadn't phoned the hospital and cursed inwardly. He couldn't let whatever was happening in his marriage distract him from his work.

'I'll do it now,' he said, pushing back his chair and standing up, although that soft touch of her hand on his might have been a prelude to—

You're losing the plot, old son, he told himself.

By the time he'd finished being switched from ward to ward and had finally found someone with enough authority to tell him how his patient really was, Fran had cleared the table, washed the dishes and was seated on a stool at the divider, frowning over another list.

She looked up expectantly.

'He's doing better than I'd hoped,' he told her, buoyed himself by the better than anticipated news. 'He was in Theatre for six hours while micro-surgeons sewed the blood vessels, nerves and sinews back together, and the ortho-pedic fellows fitted rods and plates to hold his bones to-gether. It will be a while before they know if the surgery will take, but he came through the operation better than they expected so that's a good sign.'

She looked so pleased for him he could have kissed her. In fact, he was so relieved for the man, he could have grabbed her and danced around the room. Then they—

No way! The 'keep clear' signals were unmistakable and he guessed part of being 'nice' was taking notice of such warnings. Although he suspected his 'nice' might be wear-ing thin and, where Ian Sinclair was concerned, could be-come downright nasty.

He said goodbye and walked briskly up the hill.

'Where do these Turners live?' he asked his mother, barely registering that she was surrounded by what seemed like acres of red ribbon.

'Out of town somewhere,' she said vaguely, then she smiled at him. 'I'm glad you've come. Fran's so busy I thought I'd teach you how to tie flat bows. I found all this wonderful stuff in one of our old boxes of decorations. There are other treasures as well. You should take them home with you. Fran will need them for the tree.'

'Out of town somewhere isn't very specific,' he said crossly, as once again his maternal relative swept him along a path of her own choosing.

'Well, I don't really know, dear,' she added, looking up from the ribbon in her lap and frowning slightly.

He immediately felt guilty. She'd obviously much rather fuss over ribbons and bows than answer his questions.

'It could be off the Rothbury road but I wouldn't swear to it. Are you worried about her now?'

For a split second he considered lying, but his mother had always been able to read his lies so he opted for a version of the truth.

'No, but Fran's arranged to go out to visit her and I don't want her getting lost.'

Or taking detours?

'I'm sure Mrs Stevens will give good directions. Very sensible woman, Joan Stevens. Now, the thing with these bows…'

He half listened, gathering that ordinary bows behaved badly, not sitting flat, and this particular type of bow— which apparently he was to learn to tie—would be vital for the decorating programme, and possibly the success or otherwise of the party.

'Mum, you know I'm no good at this kind of thing,' he protested when she'd pulled apart his fourth disastrous effort.

'Because you're not trying,' his mother told him. 'Your fingers are working at it but your mind's a million miles away. Fran's been looking tired lately, too. I hope you've organised a locum in the New Year so the two of you can have a proper holiday. And don't worry about leaving me. I'm going back to town with your aunts on Boxing Day. With Barney to mind the garden, I can stay with them all January.'

Griff felt a sizeable twinge of guilt. His mother had mentioned this programme some months back, even reminding him he'd have to book early to get a locum at that time of the year.

But he'd felt so relaxed and contented, so comfortable and secure in his marriage, that the thought of going anywhere, doing something different, hadn't held the slightest appeal.

'I've been bloody selfish!' he muttered to himself.

He only realised he'd spoken aloud when his mother said, 'Most people are when they're happy. It's as if bliss is a kind of cocoon that hides you away from the rest of the world. Or the rest of the world from you.'

'You're saying it excludes reality?' Griff demanded, sure this theory of his mother's couldn't possibly be true.

Could his own happiness have blinded him to unhappiness in Fran?

He considered this appalling thought and came down on the negative side. Fran *had* been happy—he was sure of it. He'd seen it in the way she'd moved, as if dancing a few inches above the ground. In the sparkle in her eyes, the tenderness in her touch—

Had been happy?

His own words came back to haunt him.

'No, that's wrong!' his mother said, but he ignored her, following his thoughts along a murky trail.

'Had been' were the key words here. But when had things changed?

'Hold the ends like this.'

Before talk of this party?

'When did Fran start looking tired?' he asked his mother, his hands pulling restlessly at another crooked bow.

'I would have thought *you'd* know that,' his parent snapped. 'Pay attention once more. Right now the bows are more important than your mental meanderings. When the party and Christmas festivities are over, Fran will have a chance to relax. Until then you should be as helpful as possible and try not to aggravate her.'

'By being nice?' Griff growled.

'Nice can be very aggravating! Now, are you watching?'

He tried again, but his mind kept seeking to unravel the knots inside his head, to make sense of the chaos that was becoming his life.

Bows, whether flat or not, seemed immaterial.

'They're beautiful, thank you,' Fran said, when Griff returned late from his mother's and presented her with a box of neat flat red ribbon bows.

'She said to tell you she has Christmas decorations as well, and that Barney was down at the nursery and says there's a perfectly shaped conifer in a pot if you want it for a living Christmas tree.'

Fran listened to the words, but it was his tone that alerted her to another shift in their relationship. He seemed to be reciting the messages, rather than talking to her, and once again a wave of sadness struck her, so fiercely all-engulfing she had to swallow hard and bend her head towards the box to hide betraying tears.

'I'll pop down to the nursery at lunchtime tomorrow,' she muttered. 'And I must remember to thank Barney.'

'We could go to the nursery together on Saturday,' Griff suggested, and Fran, who knew that the less togetherness they shared the better, reminded him she'd have the twins.

'We could all go,' he persisted. 'After morning surgery. Nurseries are great places for little kids to run around— even plant nurseries. I'll have the mobile in case I'm needed.'

Fran gave in. After all, a certain level of togetherness was inevitable in a marriage.

Perhaps it's the children thing that's bothering her, Griff decided, lying in bed much later. Fran was curled at his side, her regular breathing suggesting she was deeply asleep.

This idea was eminently more acceptable to him than thinking her preoccupation had anything to do with Ian Sinclair.

It had to be children. She's gone clucky. Why else would she have offered to take care of those two young hellions of the Smiths? From all he heard they had the energy of dynamos and could do more destruction than a couple of nuclear warheads.

Unhappiness over not conceiving—that's what was worrying her.

His thoughts twisted and turned, half-formed ideas whirling in his head.

Did knowing help?

He scanned his uneasiness and found it unabated.

Not a whit!

In fact, the statement seemed to have churned things up even more.

What if he was to blame?

Now he considered it, he was an only child of an only child on his father's side.

Weak sperm?

He groaned, and realised he'd done it aloud when a small hand reached out and soothed its way across his chest.

The touch made his heart quiver.

Or maybe the quiver was an early sign of heart disease.

His mother had heart disease.

And only one child.

Half-asleep thoughts…

Nothing making sense…

He covered the small hand with his own large one, then turned on his side, tucking his body around Fran's, careful not to wake her but needing contact, confirmation of her existence, confirmation that his marriage wasn't an illusion…

They'd adopt.

Finding so easy a solution jolted him awake, like the bump at the end of a falling sensation.

Not that adopting was easy these days.

Perhaps a sperm test first. He'd go to Toowoomba.

Or would he have to go that far?

Couldn't he do this himself?

Count the sperm?

No, an expert would do more than count. He could test for viability, motility, whatever else experts tested them for.

He tightened his hold on his wife as the random thoughts caused tremors of insecurity.

But for Fran—for the children she obviously wanted—he'd do it.

Do anything…

Damn! *He* should be the one going to the conference. A few days in Toowoomba would have been all he needed.

But she'd accepted.

Unexpectedly.

No. It had to be the conception thing worrying her, he told himself as his stomach crunched uneasily.

Go to sleep, Griff!

Thursday. Had days dragged like this before she'd come to Summerfield? She was reasonably certain it hadn't happened since then.

Today their paths had barely crossed. From Fran's early morning call to an asthmatic patient to Griff's decision to stay on at the surgery to finish an immunisation article for the paper, their working lives managed to keep them apart.

Or was it good management? Was Griff avoiding her as assiduously as she was avoiding him?

Alone in the house that evening, Fran began experimenting with the garlands she planned to hang across the windows. Her idea was to use false greenery as a base, and weave holly, ivy and red berries into it. She had stuck her finger on a holly leaf for the eighth time and was sucking at the blood when Griff came home.

'Won't those leaves be dead before the party?' he asked, waving his hand at the pile of leaves she'd gathered from Eloise's garden.

'This is a trial run,' she explained, shivering as he came closer, took her hand, examined her finger, then lifted it towards his lips.

She could feel his heat, smell his sweat, sense a tension similar to her own building in his body.

'Tired tonight?' he murmured, then his lips closed around her wounded finger, the warm moistness of his mouth and the teasing of his tongue spreading heat she didn't want to feel deep in her belly. 'Or could I interest you in a trial run of another kind?'

He gave her back her hand, with its damp digit, and drew her to him, claiming her lips before she could form words, stealing the initiative—giving her no chance to deny her body's demands.

'Your dinner's in the oven,' she reminded him, determined to at least try denial.

'No appetite for food,' he whispered, and the words coiled erotically into her ear, further weakening her resolve to keep her distance.

That was hard to do when her body was pressing ever closer to Griff's, responding to the subtle shifts of muscle, the unspoken demands. Wanting him so badly she ached with need.

So, with a tiny moan of sheer frustration, she returned his kiss, hungrily urging him on, wanting it all now she'd given in to sensation.

How they'd made it to the bedroom she wasn't sure, but much later, lying in his arms, sated and exhausted, she finally recognised her surroundings and tried to piece their movements together.

Had he carried her? Surely she'd remember—

'Well, that's still good between us.'

Griff's voice recalled her to the present. She was tucked against his side and she could feel his fingers twisting and untwisting her hair, playing with the strands, combing through it.

So sensual. So soothing. So—

'Hey! I'm talking to you. Have you gone to sleep?'

She shut her eyes tightly, hoping to squeeze the seductive power of those fingers from her consciousness. Reminded herself that it couldn't be.

Reminded herself of distance.

Of not telling Griff.

Of Plans—A and B.

'I thought it was a statement of fact,' she muttered, scrambling off the bed and reaching for her dressing gown. 'Not something that required an answer.'

She pulled the ragged garment on, finding comfort in its familiarity. Tied the belt. Tightly. She had to pull everything together—particularly her thoughts.

'I should put that greenery in water, clean up the kitchen. You'll want your dinner. Would you like a cup of tea with it or a cold drink?'

Then, without waiting for his answer, she fled.

Plan B had come to her during her short lunch-break. Meg had been talking about the conference in Toowoomba, about it being a chance for Fran to unwind after the party.

If Sheila's beautiful cousin Josie would agree to stay on—if she wasn't concerned about being alone in the house with Griff—then surely propinquity would do the rest. Wouldn't any woman spending time with Griff fall in love with him? Or at least get to know and like him enough to console him when Fran told him the marriage idea wasn't working for her?

Her stomach rolled over and her knees went shaky even thinking about that particular lie, but as no other idea had presented itself and the alternative—staying married—was so unfair to the man she loved, there was nothing else she could do.

Fran tidied up the kitchen and reheated Griff's dinner, rehashing Plan B in her head, resolutely refusing to consider why she favoured Josie over Billie Lloyd. Resolutely refusing to acknowledge her own pain.

'Don't worry about dinner. I'm going out.'

Once again Griff's voice brought her abruptly out of her reverie.

'Going out?' she echoed weakly.

'I told Melanie I'd pop in. I'll fix myself something later if I'm hungry.'

A green wave of jealousy rose up before Fran's eyes and broke across her like the pounding of the surf. It hammered in her ears and thudded in her heart, seized her lungs and sent spears of pain shooting along her nerves.

It was useless to tell herself she didn't care.

Shouldn't care.

'Melanie Miller, I assume! Naturally, popping in to see her would be far more important than eating.'

The bite of sarcasm was foreign to her tongue but she could no more prevent her anger lashing out at him than she could—

Stay with him?

'At least she's not afraid of conversation,' Griff retorted, in most un-Griff-like tones.

Then she heard him sigh, felt his hands settle on her shoulders, turn her to face him. Blue eyes looked deeply into hers. 'Shall I stay and talk to you instead?'

For a moment Fran was tempted. More than tempted, for to fling herself against his chest and sob out all her worries was what she wanted more than anything in the world.

But it was her burden, not Griff's, and telling him would mean he'd take it on his shoulders.

Then suffer for it.

'We talk all the time,' she said, aiming for casual but falling woefully short as the words trembled into nothingness. She tried again. 'Off you go. You don't want to keep Melanie waiting!'

Far better! The bite had returned to her voice and she knew he'd heard it, for his eyes hardened and his shapely lips thinned to a straight line—turning his so-familiar face into that of a stranger.

CHAPTER SEVEN

MUTED rattling noises from the kitchen brought Fran out of a heavy sleep. The coldness in the bed told her Griff was gone, but the rumpled state of the sheets suggested he'd actually shared it with her at some stage.

Unhappy over the way they'd parted—over her undeniable bitchiness—she'd lain awake for hours, wanting to apologise to him, to try to ease the tension that was not only poisoning their relationship but strangling their friendship.

Though she doubted that would survive her bombshell anyway.

Her stomach reacted as it always did to the thought of leaving Griff. It clenched and rolled and generally produced a feeling of such nausea it was all she could do to control it.

'I'm doing early calls so I'll be off!'

Her husband's voice floated up the stairs, and Fran felt her lip tremble and tears start in her eyes as she realised that was it. No goodbye kiss. No chance to make amends.

Perhaps it was for the best, she decided, brushing the tears away with the back of her hand. It would make the parting easier—make Griff less likely to argue.

Dragging a body that seemed to weigh more than an elephant into the bathroom, she showered, then walked back into the bedroom to decide what to wear.

'I couldn't go like that! With things uneasy between us.'

Griff must have seen her start when she heard his voice, or heard her little cry of surprise, for he took her naked body in his arms and held her close.

'I just want you to know, Franny, that when you *are* ready to talk about whatever's bothering you, I'm here to listen. Isn't that what friends are for?'

She had been doing all right up to the last question, when his reassertion of their 'friendship' made her heart break in two.

It was a wonder he hadn't heard the crack. Couldn't see that she was bleeding. Falling apart!

Only his arms, wrapped tightly around her, held her together. Only a mammoth effort of control stopped her howling with the pain.

Then his lips brushed against the hollow at the base of her neck, and she shivered. It would be easier to stop the sun coming up each morning than to stop her physical reactions to this man.

'It's OK for you,' Griff grumbled when she became aware his reactions were meeting and matching hers. 'You've already got your clothes off, and you're not running late for work.'

He tilted her head and kissed her firmly on the lips.

'Later!' he said huskily, and the promise in the simple, single word made her shiver.

Less togetherness, not more. Less sex, not more, she reminded herself.

But she kissed him back anyway, responding with all the hunger of her aching misery until eventually he groaned and pulled away.

'Put some clothes on, woman!' he ordered. 'Now!'

She smiled at the gruffness in his voice—and because she couldn't help but smile at this man she loved so much.

'That's my problem,' she told him. 'I've no idea what to wear. I mean, Mrs Turner hasn't been to town for maybe fifty years. Didn't people still wear hats and gloves when they went visiting back then?'

Griff grinned at her and spread his arms wide.

'Well, this is what I'm wearing if that's any help,' he said.

'What you're wearing?' Fran said hesitantly, and was surprised to see what looked like smugness in her husband's face.

'I'll explain later,' he said, then he kissed her lightly on the top of her head and left the room, clattering down the steps and out the door before she could insist on an answer.

What he'd meant, she realised when 'later' came had been that he was going with her.

'Why?' she demanded, not because she wanted less togetherness, although that was definitely a consideration, but because it was so totally unexpected. Bizarre.

Griff taking time off work? Unheard of!

'I think your community spirit must be rubbing off on me,' he said cheerfully, opening the passenger door of his car for her then belting her carefully in. 'I realise now I haven't ever done enough of that type of work.'

'You're the one who tackled the council about the immunisation programme,' Fran reminded him, whilst wondering why his explanation made her feel more, not less, uneasy.

'That's ordinary preventative medicine,' he reminded her. 'What you're doing, and reminding me of its importance, is tackling the little things in order improve people's quality of life. Which, if you think about it, is another form or preventative medicine. Relieving stress can reduce the chance of stroke or heart disease, minimise the risk of contracting other illnesses.'

They were driving down the main street, but Fran was still getting over Griff's decision to accompany her to notice much of what was happening outside.

And busy telling her body this was business, not the husband-and-wife pleasure jaunt it seemed to think it was.

'I've been remiss,' he continued.

'Nonsense!' she told him. 'You haven't had time for anything else. In fact, it's a wonder you haven't worn yourself out, running the practice single-handed for so long, taking on more and more work as the town grew.'

She saw his quick frown, but he was concentrating most of his attention on a milk tanker coming in from the Rothbury road, so she added, before he had time to protest, 'And don't tell me your father managed on his own as justification for you doing the same. When he was here, Summerfield was less than half the size it is now.'

Having successfully negotiated his way around the tanker, Griff slipped his left hand from the wheel and patted her leg.

'Good thing I finally saw the light and tracked down my best girl in that fancy clinic in Toowoomba. You didn't have time for your pastoral care work in that practice!'

'Didn't have time to learn the patients' names,' Fran agreed, trying to sound very professional while the nerve endings in the patch of skin beneath his hand tingled with automatic pleasure. Fortunately for her sanity, Griff removed his hand, needing it to steer the car through some tight curves on the road.

She took a deep breath and continued the 'professional' conversation. 'But it was a good service—providing out-of-hours consultations for people who just couldn't make normal surgery times. Or for those who got inconveniently sick when their local doctor was off duty.'

But as they continued to discuss the emergency service where she'd worked after her divorce, Fran realised just how much she enjoyed getting to know her patients as people, and working with them to promote better general health—luxuries she hadn't known at the clinic.

Yes, country practice suited her. She'd have to—

'We should be there according to the directions I got from Meg.'

As Griff's voice brought her back to the here and now, Fran looked around at the surrounding countryside.

'Mrs Stevens said there's a long drive up to the house, with huge Moreton Bay fig trees forming an arch over it. Perhaps there…'

She pointed to a patch of trees so dark a green they looked almost black from a distance.

Griff slowed the car and they peered into the thicket, finally noticing an open, lopsided gate and, beyond it, a thin dirt track disappearing into the dark shadows.

They drove through the gate and entered a different world of cool, dark gloom.

'Sleeping Beauty stuff, this,' Griff said, as the darkness increased as they travelled further down the tunnel. 'And to think I've lived here all my life and never known the place existed. I must have driven past a few hundred times and not realised there was an entrance or a house beyond the trees.'

'Within, not beyond,' Fran corrected as the drive ended abruptly, revealing a low-set, wide-verandahed house snuggled into a pretty garden, more of the big fig trees forming a protective wall all around it. 'Sleeping Beauty stuff, indeed.'

An old sedan parked at the front of the house told Fran Mrs Stevens was already there, but she felt a shiver of trepidation as she looked at the old house and considered what she was about to do.

Had Griff noticed the movement that he rested his hand on her shoulder and gave a gentle squeeze?

'It's the right thing to do, Franny,' he said, homing in on her anxiety. 'They need some other contact with the outside world for their own sakes. Imagine if something happened to Mrs Stevens.'

Fran nodded, knowing the words were true, although

they weren't doing much to settle the queasy feeling inside her. Or was Griff's touch responsible for that reaction?

She opened the door and eased herself out, conscious of a stillness in the air. But not silence. Somewhere beyond the house a rooster proclaimed his might while his womenfolk clucked and chattered.

'Fowls have such a homely sound,' Griff said, walking around the car and clasping Fran's elbow in a light yet somehow formal manner. 'Shall we go?'

They walked together to the low steps, and were almost on the verandah when the front door opened.

'Oh! There's two of you.'

The elderly woman blinked like a baby kitten unused to light.

'This is my husband...' Fran tried desperately to think of Griff's real name—the one she'd heard only on their wedding day, and had all but ruined the ceremony by laughing at it. It wouldn't come so she settled on the name she knew.

'Griff,' she said. 'Dr Griffiths.' She stepped forward and held out her hand. 'And I'm Fran.'

'We don't need one doctor, let alone two,' Mrs Turner said tartly. 'I told you that on the phone.'

'I shouldn't think so,' Griff told her, stepping forward to offer his hand. 'You look very spritely. But, as Fran explained to you, she's new in town and wanted to meet everyone. Also, Mrs Stevens is Fran's patient and Fran's a bit worried about her.'

The old lady frowned. And well she might, Fran thought. Talk about coming directly to the point!

'Joan? You're here to talk about Joan?'

Griff murmured something Fran failed to hear, and bent solicitously over Mrs Turner, suggesting perhaps they move inside, sit down, be comfortable.

And Mrs Turner fell for his charm, smiling at him, turning to lead them down a short, dark hall.

Whatever works, Fran decided as she followed the pair into a formal sitting room with timber-panelled walls and heavy furniture covered in a faded Regency-striped material. Griff's hand wrapped around her wrist and guided her towards the couch.

'You'll have tea?' their hostess asked, her voice surprisingly strong for a nonagenarian.

Fran was startled by the offer from a woman who obviously wanted as little as possible to do with them.

'Oh, no,' she began.

'Thank you, we'd certainly appreciate a cuppa.' Griff cut across her negative reply, then grinned apologetically at her as Mrs Turner left the room, returning only a minute later.

'Albert will see to it,' she said, and settled herself on one of the chairs. 'Albert is my son, but I suppose Joan told you that. Joan fusses about Albert but he's perfectly capable of looking after himself. Looks after me as well.'

Fran weighed up the words while Griff made admiring remarks about the splendour of the old trees and the condition of the even older house.

Mrs Turner was playing the part of the gracious hostess as if she entertained on a daily basis. Perhaps, as local aristocracy, she had.

So why stop? Why become a recluse?

To hide a child who was born different?

That answer didn't seem as likely now she'd heard Mrs Turner speak of her son.

A shuffling noise broke into Fran's mental cogitations and she looked up to see a stocky, solid-looking man enter the room, the tea-tray in his hands perfectly balanced, despite its load of shiny silver teapot, delicate china cups and saucers and a plate of fresh-baked scones.

'This is my son Albert,' Mrs Turner said, and the pride

in her voice stirred more doubt in Fran's mind, while her medical self was busy diagnosing. Tight curling grey hair, not unusual in itself, but put together with low set ears and a slightly webbed neck. It was a fairly obscure syndrome. Turner's?

She didn't think so. Probably word association!

Albert sent a shy smile in her direction but she could sense his tension.

Griff had stood up and moved forward, waiting until Albert had set the tray down on a small table before introducing himself. Now he waved his hand towards a chair, obviously asking the man to join them.

'Tea with Joan,' Albert said, nodding his head to indicate the nether regions of the house where Mrs Stevens must have been working. He hurried off, no doubt pleased to escape the strangers.

'I hope we'll see you again before we go,' Griff called after him, then he turned back to Mrs Turner. 'And as I'm on my feet, shall I be mother?'

Mrs Turner looked confused.

'Pour the tea?' Griff translated for her, then he smiled and Fran saw the older woman respond with a faint smile of her own.

'Be mother indeed!' she said. 'Yes, make yourself useful. Go ahead and pour.'

She watched him as he fussed over the tray, something so akin to wariness in her eyes that Fran was puzzled.

Then, as Griff set the cup and saucer and plate on the small table beside their hostess's chair and Mrs Turner reached out a hand to take a scone, Fran noticed the misshapen arm.

Somewhere along the track—in her years of reclusive living—she'd broken a bone and not had it correctly set.

'You're worried about Joan.'

It was Mrs Turner who brought the subject back to business.

'Not so much worried as concerned she doesn't overdo things,' Fran said gently. 'Her arthritis is quite severe and when it flares up, holding anything in her hand, even a toothbrush, is painful.'

'She didn't tell me,' Mrs Turner said. 'Not that I'd expect her to. They're uncomplaining women, those Turners. Her mother was the same. Never a word of complaint. They've both been good to me—very good, considering.'

She sipped at her tea, her rheumy eyes unfocussed as she followed through unspoken thoughts.

'I can arrange to have home help for you,' Fran said. 'Someone coming in once a week to do the work Mrs Stevens does. Meals delivered as well, if you think you'd like that.'

Focus returned and Mrs Turner shook her head very firmly.

'I can still cook meals, my girl,' she said. 'And Albert helps. It takes him a while to learn things, but once he learns he never forgets. In fact, he's turned out to be a better baker than I am. A lighter touch. He cooked these scones.'

'They're delicious,' Griff told her. 'I can cook plain meals, but fancy things like scones—count me out.'

'You cook meals? For your wife?'

Mrs Turner's surprise was almost comical.

'We both work the same hours so why should Fran have to do all the cooking?' Griff responded. 'We take turns, although, I must admit, things she cooks always taste better.'

'And meals you cook taste better to me,' Fran reminded him. 'I think there's always more appeal in food you don't have to cook yourself.'

As she spoke, she was aware of Mrs Turner watching their exchange, something like sadness in her face.

'But that's not why we're here,' she said, shifting the conversation firmly back to the subject of home help. 'Do you think you could accept someone else bringing out your shopping and doing some housework for you? Mrs Stevens could show them what to do, how you like things done. Even supervise for the first few weeks.'

Fran sat back, aware she shouldn't push too hard, biting back her opinion that it might be good for Albert to have more contact with the outside world.

'Would the person who came have to report to someone?'

Report to someone? Translated, it could mean talk about them. That was more likely to be Mrs Turner's concern— the gossip she'd been at such pains to avoid for so long.

'The service is organised by Lucy Crane. She keeps tabs on the hours all the helpers work, sees to their pay, things like that. She might like to visit you first if that was acceptable to you, but the person assigned to assist you is bound by the rules of the service to respect your confidentiality and your privacy. You wouldn't have to worry that someone could spread stories about your home or your personal lives.'

'Would it only be for me?' Mrs Turner asked, after a pause so long that Griff had demolished two scones and poured himself a second cup of tea. Talk about making himself at home!

'It's a service offered to a lot of people,' Fran said. 'Anyone who can't manage everything on their own, but who wants to remain living in their own home rather than go into a hostel or aged care facility.'

'But out here,' Mrs Turner persisted. 'Would someone keep coming all this way, even if I wasn't here? When I'm dead.'

She said the words with defiance, as though challenging the fates to take her if they dared.

'Would they keep coming for Albert?' Griff said. 'Is that what's worrying you?'

Mrs Turner nodded, and Fran could see the moisture in her eyes.

'Of course,' she said quickly. 'That's one of the reasons it might be good to start now, so Albert can get used to other people being here, and get to know them. Not that you don't look good for another ten years at least.'

The old woman smiled at her.

'I won't need ten if I know Albert's all right. I've tried to train him, and I knew Joan was getting older, wouldn't be able to cope for ever...'

'He could go and live in town,' Griff said, once again coming bluntly to the point. 'In a hostel or with Mrs Stevens. She indicated to Fran that she'd enjoy the company.'

Griff spoke gently, but Fran could see the final words had gone right over Mrs Turner's head. Her skin had blanched when Griff had mentioned town and her lips trembled, as if she was having trouble keeping back her tears.

'But someone might take him away,' she whimpered.

Fran stood up and crossed to sit on the arm of Mrs Turner's chair. She put her arm around the older woman's shoulders.

'No, they wouldn't,' she assured her. 'Being different isn't a crime. Albert is a fine, upstanding man, with skills a lot of men his age don't have. These days, when children with special needs are born, society accepts them. They aren't sent away to homes or institutions, but brought up with their siblings, going to regular schools in most cases. They act in plays, enjoy sporting activities, even have their own Olympic Games. Who knows, maybe if he lives in town, Albert might take up lawn bowls or some other game, become a champion.'

'I wouldn't let them put him in a home! When he was

born everyone said I had to, but I wouldn't sign the papers.'
Mrs Turner whispered her confession, then she looked up
at Fran, her tired eyes awash with tears. 'I was right, wasn't
I?'

Fran smiled and blinked her own watery eyes.

'Exactly right,' she said briskly. 'And way ahead of your
time as far as keeping him at home is concerned.'

From her vantage point on the arm of the chair, she could
see an ugly, ridged scar running across the woman's scalp,
clearly visible through the thinning hair. Another untreated
wound.

Mrs Turner obviously loved her son very dearly but had
she remained immured in this house for so many years for
some reason other than his disability? And keeping him
safe from the authorities?

Fran shivered as a dark shadow of an idea crossed her
mind. Surely not!

Griff had taken up the conversational ball and was now
talking cheerfully about other things Albert could do if or
when he shifted into town.

'Yes, he'd like that.' Mrs Turner agreed with Griff's latest suggestion and Fran sensed she wasn't as concerned
about Albert's eventual 'coming out' as they'd expected her
to be. Or as she had been earlier. Perhaps now the spectre
of the institution had been lifted, she'd been relieved of a
worry she hadn't been able to share with anyone.

Mrs Stevens came in a few minutes later, followed by
Albert.

'He'd like to show you the fowls and the garden,' Mrs
Stevens said, while Albert echoed some of the words and
again smiled shyly.

Noonan's syndrome. The words flashed in Fran's mind.
Some sufferers were very high achievers, their disability
only obvious in physical manifestations. Others were less
able—poor co-ordination, little speech.

With Albert that could be from his isolation.

Her mind was busy filling in the blanks as she followed Griff and Albert through a kitchen redolent with the smell of baking. It was like something out of an old movie. Big oak dressers stacked with crockery. An ancient but obviously still functioning wood stove, its enamel gleaming cleanly. A black kettle sat at the back, steaming slightly— hot water at the ready. A tap above an old porcelain sink was some concession to mod cons!

Yet the house had the telephone and electricity connected. The late Mr Turner must have seen fit to install these conveniences, so why not an electric stove?

Probably because it wasn't something he considered necessary to his own comfort.

'Out here,' Albert said, and they followed him into the back yard where neat raised garden beds were planted with rows of healthy tomatoes, carrots and lettuce.

'Chooks!'

Albert waved his hand towards a sturdy hen house and wire netting run. It was clean and dry, with a bunch of fresh thistles tucked into the wire and a scatter of dandelion leaves on the ground.

'Chooks eat wheat seeds,' Albert added, opening a door behind the run, and showing them drums of seed.

'Who brings the feed out from town?' Griff asked.

'Joan. Joan likes chooks. I give her eggs.'

It was simple conversation, but forming ideas into sentences and linking them together showed that Albert was probably intelligent enough to function on his own.

But out here? With no company?

'Do you think he'd understand the concept of death?' Fran asked when she and Griff, after a guided tour of the property and farewells all round, were driving back to town.

'As in being on his own when his mother dies?'

'Precisely,' Fran said.

She looked at her husband's familiar profile and felt her heart quail at the thought of leaving him.

'I don't think we need to worry about that right now. You've succeeded in getting her to agree to home help—'

'You succeeded,' Fran reminded him. 'Leaping right to the point. I'd probably still be sitting there, nursing my fifth cup of tea and wondering how to bring up the subject.'

'Well, she had a sensible look about her. As if she knew what was what. I took the risk that a direct approach might work.'

'And it did,' Fran mused. 'But it doesn't gel with her not going to town after Albert was born. Protecting him from public view. She seems so sensible in other ways. Proud of him...'

'She was clearly upset about institutionalisation. Although she'd refused to sign the papers, would she have kept him at home to avoid the subject coming up again?'

Fran thought for a moment.

'Perhaps so, especially if someone was reinforcing that threat.'

'What's on your mind?'

Fran shrugged, then said hesitantly, 'Did you notice her arm?'

'Broken but not set properly? Taking her avoidance of going to town to extremes? Are you thinking agoraphobia?'

Fran shook her head.

'No. Though agoraphobia's a silly word, isn't it? I mean, something that describes fear of open spaces as well as fear of crowded places. Surely if you feared one, the other would represent safety?'

Actually, what she was thinking was so upsetting she was pleased to be discussing something else.

'So what *are* you thinking?'

Trust Griff not to take the hint.

'She mentioned the Turner women being uncomplaining

folks. So Mrs Stevens's mother must have been a Turner, making her Mrs Turner's sister-in-law.'

They were out of the dark tunnel now, so she saw the sparkle in Griff's eyes as he flashed a cheeky grin her way.

'I assume this investigation of the family tree is leading somewhere?'

'I was wondering about Mr Turner,' she told him, her voice soft as she remembered statistics she'd read in a recent medical journal.

Griff's face darkened and she knew he'd caught at least a glimmer of her thoughts.

'What did that article say? Something about a hidden epidemic? That spousal abuse was equally prevalent in country areas yet rarely reported?'

'Your mother said he was aristocracy in the town. And Mrs Turner was used to entertaining. Do you think a baby who wasn't quite right—particularly a son she refused to institutionalise—would make more of a mark on a man like that?'

Griff shook his head.

'We can't assume that, but from the way Mrs Turner spoke she was under some pressure. After all, Albert must be close to sixty. It would have been considered the way to go in those days.'

'Good for her, but maybe she suffered for it. It could have been the father who didn't want people staring.'

'Or didn't want people seeing the damage he could do to his wife,' Griff said grimly.

They were back in town and he steered the car deftly into their small car park. He pulled on the handbrake, switched off the engine, but didn't move.

'Pure speculation, isn't it, Franny? And we'll probably never know the truth. But at least you've broken through the barrier, and let Mrs Turner know there are more people than Joan Stevens she can call on for help.'

He leant across the console between them and kissed her gently on the cheek. Then, with his hand cupping her chin, he lifted a stray strand of her hair and tucked it behind her ear. Blue eyes looked deeply into hers.

'We all need to know there's someone there for us,' he said, his voice rich with an emotion she couldn't identify. 'I'm your someone, Fran Griffiths. Remember that!'

Fran tried frantically to swallow the huge lump that had formed in her throat. And hoped her watery eyes weren't giving her away.

She clasped her arms around her body, trying to rid herself of an almost overwhelming need to cry, then turned away from him, dipping her head and hunching her shoulders, hoping to hide the moisture leaking from beneath her tightly closed eyelids.

A car door opening told her Griff had moved, and she froze in the seat, wondering if he was walking around the car. Would be witness to her silent despair. But his footsteps crunched across the gravel and she heard the automatic front doors hiss open.

'I'm your someone,' he'd said. Words so reassuring she should have been pleased.

So why did they make the pain worse? Why was she so foolish as to wish he'd offered some other sentiment?

Like love!

CHAPTER EIGHT

IT WAS Fran's last moment of weakness. Reminding herself firmly that the main reason her plan would work was because Griff *didn't* love her, and that she should be pleased, not maudlin, over it, she turned her attention to work, and in every spare minute to planning the upcoming festivities.

With the conference in Toowoomba beginning the Monday after the party, and Christmas Day only a few days after her return, she'd have to have most of her Christmas preparations in hand before she left.

Then there was the immunisation programme.

Not to mention the twins.

'I'll be home at lunchtime to give you a hand with them,' Griff reminded her when they were dawdling over breakfast. Saturday surgery didn't begin until nine and the phone had been blessedly silent.

'Don't rush through your appointments on my account. I'm sure I'll be able to manage.'

Griff raised his eyebrows and smiled, and Fran knew it was because she'd had to drag herself forcibly out of bed. Her body seemed to resent this change in the routine as if it knew that every second Saturday it got to lie in until later. Even now, after coffee instead of her usual juice, she was feeling lethargic.

'What's the plan?'

Anxious to hide how she felt from her husband, she tried a bright smile.

'I thought the park first. I'll take some juice and sandwiches so we can have a little picnic, then go across from there to the nursery. I'll have their stroller so we can walk, and hopefully they might fall asleep for a while. Then home for a rest, and a visit to your mother's garden for an hour or so before I drop them back to Jenny.'

'Given the pair's reputation, you'll be exhausted before you finish the first part of the exercise. I'll meet you at the nursery. I'll fit the children's car seats from the surgery so we can all drive back home from there.'

'That would be great,' Fran told him. The way she was feeling, she was too grateful for his promise of assistance to worry about the togetherness aspect of the expedition.

She stood up and began to prepare the picnic, accepted Griff's goodbye kiss with the usual tremor of delight, agreed she'd see him later, then, after smothering herself with sunscreen before adding the bottle to the supplies in her small backpack, she set out.

The morning wasn't as bad as she'd expected. With so much to do, so much space to occupy, the twins managed to stay out of mischief—if you didn't count having to be rescued from the low branch of a tree, or stopped from going up the slide part of the slippery dip, or fighting with other children who dared to share the roundabout with them.

'Now, when we've had our lunch we're going to walk across the park to the nursery. That's a shop where you can buy all kinds of plants and trees.'

She wasn't sure how much they understood but she felt better sharing each stage of her plan with them. At this pronouncement, two sets of dark eyes looked up at her, and two little heads nodded in unison. Fran felt the pain of regret twist in her belly as she considered her own childless state.

Everything went according to plan until they reached the nursery, where the pots of bright colour attracted the twins' grasping hands. As Fran rescued a red petunia from Sean, Grant reached for a blue one.

'Aha! Beauty in distress.'

Fran looked up to see Ian Sinclair laughing at her from further along the aisle of pots.

'More like a lonely little onion in a petunia patch,' she grumbled, then she launched herself around the awkward stroller to save another pot. 'No, Sean. You mustn't touch it, darling.'

'Perhaps I can help,' Ian suggested. 'What if I drive, and you do the policing?'

He came up the aisle and seized the handle at the back of the stroller.

'Where are you heading?'

'Towards the conifers but I've no idea where to find them. I don't come in here that often. Barney grows most of Eloise's annuals from seeds and hands on a few seed-lings to me every now and then. Anything else I want I pinch as cuttings from her garden.'

'It's a splendid place,' Ian agreed, steering the twins competently out of the petunia display and down a wider aisle where the only things to tempt their hands were huge and virtually indestructible terracotta pots.

Fran felt sufficiently at ease to walk beside him.

'Why the conifers?' Ian asked.

'I wanted something for a Christmas tree,' Fran said. 'I wanted to have a tree up in time for the party, and as the Rotary Club doesn't begin to sell their trees until the last week I thought I'd see about a live one. Actually, Barney suggested it.'

They reached the display of pine trees which also seemed hardy enough to resist the twins' grasping hands.

'Are you looking for something in particular?' Ian asked as they wound their way through what was virtually a maze of potted pines of every description. Tall ones were set on the ground, smaller ones on benches, so eight-foot high walls of sweet-scented greenery hemmed them in. 'Does size matter to you? Height?'

Griff, arriving only slightly late and heading immediately towards the conifer section, heard the question and recognised Ian Sinclair's voice.

It's coincidence, he told himself when he heard his wife's chuckle.

'What a question,' she said, in a teasing voice Griff hadn't heard for some time.

His stomach tensed and he bit back the growl that wanted to burst from his lips.

Damn the man! It had to be Ian pushing this relationship. After all, Fran hadn't shown the slightest interest in Sinclair's place when they'd driven past the previous day. Hadn't even glanced in that direction.

Fran was saying something else, but speaking in a low voice so Griff missed the content of the words.

Or most of them.

One word—'darling'—came through loud and clear, and the knots in his stomach tightened. He clenched his fists and held his breath, summoning all his self-control to prevent his body hurling itself through the imprisoning trees to slug the slimy vet!

Two strides took him to the end of the row, then he turned in the direction of his wife's voice and plunged down another alley.

'Ah! There you are!' he said, with masterful restraint.

Fran, who was kneeling in front of the twins' stroller, finished untangling the fingers of one of the children from a plant before turning to greet him, but the rat-fink Sinclair had the hide to smile.

Covering his guilt, Griff decided, although, as far as he could tell, the man looked more relieved than guilty.

'Oh, Griff! You've arrived!'

Fran straightened up and all but fell into his arms, hugging him tightly, apparently more delighted than chagrined.

Not that he was fooled by this display of wifely appreciation. For one thing, their caresses had been few and far between lately, so this public show of affection was suspicious in itself!

'If you could watch the children and keep them from denuding the lower branches of leaves, I'll be able to look at the trees.' She smiled at him. 'I hadn't realised taking twins to a nursery was a three-man job!'

Restraining another growl, Griff came closer, nodding a curt greeting to Ian before positioning himself beside the stroller.

'Let's go,' he said, although what he *wanted* to do was throw his wife over his shoulder and get out of this place.

Perhaps it was the jungle atmosphere…

'Hey. Stop that!'

Griff roared the command, then hopped up and down as he tried to rub his wounded leg.

Fran spun back towards him, alarm on her face, and both twins began to bellow.

Ignoring his pain, she again dropped to her knees, reaching out to pat the blond heads and reassure the small children.

'There there, darlings,' she murmured. 'Griff didn't mean to yell.'

'Of course I meant to yell!' Griff muttered. 'One of them just pulled a hundred hairs out of my leg. You'd roar, too, if it happened to you.'

'I thought the words of that old song went, "You would *cry* too if it happened to you."'

This snide interjection from Ian Sinclair didn't help. In fact, it made Griff want to haul back and hit him.

'There, there, babies. It's OK. Would you like something to drink?'

The twins had quietened, and Fran was rummaging around in the bottom compartment of the stroller. Eventually, she produced an insulated container and opened it to reveal two bottles of milk.

Four chubby hands reached eagerly towards the bottles, and as soon as they had grasped their drinks the two settled back in the stroller, sucking thirstily.

'I was trying to keep the bottles until they lay down for a rest,' Fran said worriedly. She turned to Ian. 'Do you know anything about toddlers? Will they still have a sleep if they don't have their bottles to soothe them?'

Ian held up his hands in dismay.

'Calves I can handle, but babies? No way!' He nodded towards Griff. 'Don't doctors know this stuff?'

'Not the practical everyday things,' Fran said, and Griff sensed she was genuinely concerned. 'Perhaps I should forget about the tree and take them home so they can have their sleep now.'

She gave a distracted look around.

'The trees seem very expensive anyway.'

'Why don't you come out to my place later today or tomorrow?' Ian suggested. 'The property on Rothbury road, not the veterinary clinic. I've a stand of pines out on the back boundary. Legacy of one of those pine plantations started back in the fifties. That's where the Rotary Club gets its supply for sale each year. Come this weekend to have a look, then, if there's nothing suitable, you have the option of this place to fall back on.'

Ian was speaking to both of them, *and* making sense. Though perhaps he was seeking an easy way to escape from what was now an awkward threesome.

But if he thought Griff was going to let Fran go out there alone…

'That's a wonderful idea,' Fran was saying. 'Not today.

I'll keep the twins as long as I can, although perhaps taking them for a drive—'

'No!' Griff said. 'By the time they've had a sleep and we've been up to see Mum, you'll have given Jenny a really decent break. Can you imagine them out on a farm, with cattle to annoy, dams to fall into?'

He saw Fran shudder and shake her head, agreeing with him that it was too terrible to contemplate. He turned his attention to Ian.

'We can come tomorrow. Would any particular time suit you?'

Ian shrugged.

'I don't have to be there,' he said. 'You know my place. Don't take the first entrance, take the second, over the ramp then straight on for about a kilometre. There's a gate on the right and you go through that then straight across country to the trees.'

Griff studied the other man as he gave his directions. If he was disappointed not to be getting Fran out there on her own, he wasn't showing it.

'Actually,' Ian continued, apparently unaware of Griff's scrutiny, 'if you can manage on your own I'd be very grateful. I've a hell of a lot of work to do over this next week.'

Maybe he took Griff's continued assessment for interest, for he added, 'I'm off to Toowoomba the following week. Right after the firefighters' dance, in fact. This year, I'm taking a whole month off over Christmas. I've got a locum coming in.'

They were all moving towards the exit and Griff heard all the words, although his mind had seized on one phrase in particular—the part where Ian mentioned Toowoomba in conjunction with the timing of his holiday. Straight after the dance!

Exactly when Fran was heading for the garden city!

Again, his physical reaction was so strong it startled him.

Apart from causing a bit of talk in the small town, would hitting the man right now provoke much trouble?

A possible lawsuit prevented him from taking the action his body longed for, and he unclenched his fists and forced himself to act normally.

If only he could remember how!

'Griff?'

Fran's anxious voice penetrated the red mists of frustrated rage.

'Are you all right?'

Her hand gripped his forearm, and her dark eyes peered worriedly up into his face.

'Fine! Thinking of something else. Did you say something?'

She nodded, then, her anxiety obviously not allayed, said, 'I think I'll walk the twins home. They're both asleep and moving them into the car seats then out again when we get home would probably wake them.'

'Applies to children, too, the sleeping dog thing?' Ian said lightly. 'As I've got the knack of steering this thing now, how about I push them home for you?'

Griff's blood pressure rose again when he realised he'd been outmanoeuvred. But he hadn't lost. Not yet.

'No way, mate!' he said briskly. 'You've just been telling us how busy you are. Thanks for giving Fran a hand until I arrived but, now I'm here, off you go to tackle whatever you have to do. And thanks for the offer of a tree.'

Griff eased Ian away from the controls of the stroller, then remembered he'd come by car. He fished in his pocket for the keys and tossed them to his wife.

'You've probably had enough exercise for the week after taking these two to the park. Why don't you drive home?'

The ploy should have worked perfectly, but he'd barely begun to push the stroller towards the exit than he heard

Fran say, 'Did you walk down, Ian? Can I give you a lift somewhere?'

Offering someone a lift was a perfectly normal, neighbourly thing to do, he told himself as he pushed the stroller at a savage clip along the pavement. An offer he'd probably have made himself if he'd been the one driving home.

And if he hadn't been so darned suspicious!

'Do you think if I leave them in the stroller they'll have a proper sleep?'

Fran was waiting for him by the front gate, a worried frown puckering her brow as she surveyed the sleeping children.

'They'll have more of a sleep than if you try to put them on a bed,' he told her. Then, because she still looked worried, and he hated seeing her worried, he added, 'Wasn't going up to visit Mum part of your grand plan for the day? What if we do that now? Keep walking them. That way they're sure to stay asleep.'

She smiled gratefully and fell in beside him, but suspicions didn't vanish because the object of them was no longer around.

'Drop Ian back at work?' Griff found himself asking, his tone so noncommittal he added silent congratulations to himself.

'No, downtown,' Fran said easily. 'He'd gone up to the nursery in search of some obscure poison he thought might be included in one of their garden insecticides, but when he found they didn't have it was going to try the hardware store.'

'Obscure poison?' Images of movies he'd seen where a lover murdered his love object's spouse rose obligingly in Griff's head.

'Something to do with the summer flea plague,' Fran expanded. 'Apparently, the level of toxicity in most flea rinses has been reduced to make them safer for the dogs, and to reduce the spread of more deadly chemicals in the environment.'

Deadly?

'And Ian's trying to buy the old toxic stuff in some other form? Is that what you mean?'

Fran shook her head and the thick braid in which she'd tied her hair this morning came flopping over her shoulder, making her look about sixteen.

A sexy sixteen!

'He lost a dog yesterday afternoon. The owner brought it in very sick and in the end Ian couldn't save it. The owner swore it hadn't eaten anything, and had been fine one minute then went into convulsions the next. According to Ian, the dog had been bathed that day, and the smell of insecticide in its coat made him think of poison, although the owner denied using anything strong on the animal.'

Griff was drawn into the problem in spite of his anger against the man.

'So Ian's checking out what's available locally that might kill both fleas and dogs?'

Humans as well? the suspicion he couldn't control suggested.

'Exactly!' Fran said, then she waved towards his mother who was sitting in her usual position on the verandah, and abandoned him and the children to hurry up the stairs.

'Oh, the sweet things!' his mother cooed, peering down to where he was trying to work out how women negotiated stairs with a contraption like the one in his control. 'Why don't you take them around the back? You'll be able to get into the greenhouse as it's all flat. It will be nice and cool in there for them.'

He saw Fran shudder.

'Not the greenhouse, Eloise,' she said quickly. 'If they happen to wake up, they'll tear the ferns apart in next to no time.'

'Not if Griff's watching them,' his mother said serenely. She waved him towards the path that led around to the back of the house, then turned to Fran. 'I guess you could do with a cup of tea. Come on in.'

It was a conspiracy, that's what it was, Griff decided as he pushed the stroller along the designated route.

'Don't let anyone ever tell you it's a man's world, chums,' he told the sleeping babies. 'From time to time we might be allowed to think we've won a skirmish, but the big battles of the war between the sexes usually go to the females of our species.'

The twins slept on, oblivious to his dark philosophical comments.

He turned the stroller to face the small garden seat his mother had installed in a fern-shaded grotto, and sat where he could 'watch' the pair.

'Here, I've brought you some tea and freshly baked sultana cake, and if you want to go in and talk to your mother I'll keep an eye on them now.'

Fran spoke quietly, pulling him out of a kind of limbo that was not yet sleep but coming close.

'No. I'm happy here,' he told her, then he patted the bench invitingly. 'Room for two.'

Her dark eyes seemed to sparkle, as if the invitation pleased her, then the lights went out and she shook her head with an unexpected firmness.

'No, I'd better check out what's flowering in the garden. That's why I came after all. And next week we'll be busy with the after-hours programme and getting the house ready.'

He took the tea and the plate with two fat wedges of cake, and put them on the seat where he'd hoped his wife might sit.

'Off you go, then,' he said, although his heart was behaving badly, thudding in his chest as if his wife's flurry of excuses had been a grim portent of some kind.

Back at home an hour later, he watched as she stripped off grubby clothes and bathed the sturdy little bodies. Her hands were gentle, yet always in control, her voice soft with affection as she talked reassuringly to the children, telling them little stories, laughing and joking with them.

In the end he walked away, making an excuse about some paperwork he needed to do, heading for their study because watching her with the toddlers made his heart ache with an unaccustomed pain.

And if he felt like that, how must Fran feel? He'd used the lure of having babies together to talk her into marrying him, and he'd failed her.

No! He didn't know that yet. Although her failure to conceive *must* be worrying Fran.

Should he bring up the subject?

How?

His thought processes were still in disarray. Whenever he tried to think, he heard Ian's question—and the mumble of Fran's reply. The endearment!

'I'll push them home in the stroller,' he offered when she had them dried and dressed and, by the look in the two pairs of bright eyes, raring to go again. 'That way, you can have a long relaxing bath and a rest. Later, we might go down to the pub for dinner to save either of us cooking.'

Fran smiled at him.

'Sounds just great to me,' she said. 'And if you take a circuitous route, you'll give Jenny a few extra minutes of peace, although, knowing her, she's probably missing the little devils by now.'

She kissed both the boys, and made smooching noises at them, calling them her little darlings in a soft, cooing kind of voice. But she didn't seem to think a walk down the street warranted a goodbye kiss for her husband.

Taking this as another sign of the deterioration of their marriage, Griff worried over it as he took the children home, working himself into what was perilously close to a sulk by the time he returned to the house. Where his wife lay sleeping so soundly she didn't stir as he walked in, didn't move as he sat down heavily on the edge of the bed, then lay back, staring at the ceiling, the sulk forgotten as the sight of her serene face, with its pale pink lips, straight nose and eyelash-shadowed cheeks stirred other emotions within him.

He fell asleep himself, waking to darkness and a slim, warm body curled against him. Her steady, slightly noisy breathing told him she was still deeply asleep, and he knew it would be cruel to wake her, although he ached with wanting her and longed for the reassurance of their togetherness which he imagined love-making would bestow on him.

Easing himself out of the bed, he tucked a light blanket around her and left her to the dreams he couldn't share.

'You should have woken me,' Fran told him the next morning. 'Weren't we going out for dinner? Heavens! I slept for fourteen straight hours. No one needs that much sleep. Although, if it hadn't been for the hunger pains, who knows how long I might have stayed there?'

She had finished her cereal and was on to toast by the time Griff joined her. He was rumpled from sleep, still heavy-eyed, as if his night had been as bad as hers had been good.

'Did you have a late call? Did I sleep through that as well?'

'No!' He shook his head as if to underline the statement, but offered no other reason for his tiredness, and Fran put insidious thoughts of Melanie Miller right out of her head.

'So, what time would you like this drive in the country?'

The question made Fran frown.

'Drive in the country?' she repeated.

'To Ian's place, to look for a Christmas tree.'

Griff's voice had an edge of exaggerated patience, and once again Fran peered closely at her husband, wondering just why he was so edgy.

Although, in some ways, edgy was good. He'd be far less likely to object to her leaving if he was at odds with her. Far more likely to succumb to the charms of Josie.

Or Jill.

Or Tina.

'The earlier the better, as far as I'm concerned,' she answered belatedly. 'Once I've sorted out what I'm doing about a tree, it will be one more thing crossed off the list.'

Griff had poured himself some coffee and was hunched moodily over it, and something in the way he sat reminded her of little Sean the day before when he'd slipped off the swing and bumped his bottom. He'd cried out for his mother then realised she wasn't there, and the lost look on his face had cut deeply into Fran's heart.

She stood up to take her dirty plate to the sink, then turned and put her arms around her husband.

'I'm sorry I spoiled our evening,' she said, pressing her lips against the softness of his hair. 'Not a very good afternoon off for you, was it?'

He turned his head so their lips met, and he kissed her very gently.

For some reason, the tenderness of it made Fran want to cry. So much so that she had to blink hard and detach herself—move away—before he saw her pathetic reaction and wondered at it.

'And I haven't come up with any solution for Jenny and other young mothers like her,' she said, facing the sink, away from Griff, and wiping her eyes with the backs of her hands. 'Unless…' She spun back to face him as the idea came hurtling out of nowhere. Possibly her subconscious had been working overtime to think of anything but Griff!

'Do you think we might be able to talk someone like the community welfare officer at the council into organising some kind of babysitting club? I've heard of them working in other places. Young mothers minding each other's children, collecting points. I realise Jenny couldn't take on any more at the moment but, once this baby's born, would it be much worse having four littlies running around for a few hours than three?'

Griff smiled at her, which sent her heart into palpitations despite the fact it knew it shouldn't be reacting to his smiles. She'd had any number of stern conversations with it on the subject.

'From Christmas trees to babysitting. Does your mind never rest? Could we have a moratorium on good works and the social issues of Summerfield just for one day?'

He spoke lightly but Fran heard tension in the words and realised that since she'd begun to plan her departure she'd used 'issues', as Griff put it, to mask her own anxiety and distance herself from the man she loved.

'Deal!' she said, although she knew relaxing her guard wasn't a good idea. But with only one week to go before the party—and a busy week at that—surely she was entitled to a little fun.

A day off from her campaign of distance?

A day to make memories she could treasure for ever?

CHAPTER NINE

THEY drove out along the road they'd taken on the previous Friday.

'I know I've been to Ian's place before, but I hadn't realised it was along this road,' Fran said, as Griff pointed out the first gate and asked her to keep an eye out for the second.

Having given in to temptation, she was feeling light-hearted, and the blue sky above, the warm sunshine, the rolling, grass-clad hills were all conspiring to make her feel relaxed.

'There!'

She pointed, and as her hand was over that way she let it stay there, resting on Griff's shoulder. What she really wanted to do was snuggle up to him—like a teenager out with her first love—but if she undid her seat belt and leant across to put her arms around him, he'd probably think she was mad!

She'd have to make do with looking at him—imprinting every detail of his face on her mind so she could keep that much of him with her for ever.

They bumped across the grid and followed the faint marks of tyre tracks across the grassy paddock.

'He said a kilometre. Can you see any trees?'

The question made Fran look around. She'd been far too busy cataloguing the way Griff's eyebrows grew to have taken much notice of scenery.

'Perhaps we're on the wrong property,' she said, but at that moment they crested a small hill and there, in the hollow beneath them, the plantation of pine trees spread like a darker green quilt across the grass.

'It looks like something out of a fairy-tale—an enchanted forest,' Fran said, when Griff stopped the car in the shade of the nearest trees.

'Didn't the big bad wolf live in one of those fairy-tale forests?' Griff asked.

For a moment Fran was startled out of her determination to make the most of the day, then she looked into the cool green aisles between the trees and decided that no amount of uncharacteristic Griff-grumpiness was going to spoil her day.

She slid an arm around her husband's shoulders and rested her head against his.

'Then it's a good thing I've got a handsome prince like you to protect me,' she said, and nuzzled her nose against his ear.

He turned his head and their lips met, only this time she didn't pull away. This time she kissed him back, desperation giving an edge to her hunger for him, demanding everything he had to give.

'I'd forgotten how uncomfortable kissing in cars could be,' he eventually muttered.

'I put a blanket in the boot with the picnic basket. Want to try out the enchanted forest?'

She knew she'd surprised him when he eased back and looked deep into her eyes, but she didn't want to talk. She wanted action. She wanted to lose herself, blot out her pain and despair, in the physical sensations only this man could provide.

So she kissed him again because that meant she could close her eyes and hide her thoughts. Only this time it was a tempting kiss that left his lips and trailed down the strong column of his neck, before tangling in the fine whorls of hair on his chest.

'Enough, my fairy princess! Let's explore your forest.'

Griff stopped her seductive exploration with his gruff command, but she smiled when he went immediately to the boot, picked up both the picnic basket and the blanket then led the way into the darkest of the shadows.

Pine needles crackled underfoot as she followed him, and the fresh scent drenched the air. Left untended, young trees had sprouted beneath the old ones, causing thickets in places.

'Here?' Griff turned towards her, his free hand indicating a secluded glade.

'No big bad wolf in sight?' Fran teased, and her heart raced when she saw his smile and realised he was entering into her fantasy.

'Only one!' he growled, setting the picnic basket down on the ground and spreading the blanket beside it. 'And he's a very domesticated wolf so you have nothing to fear.'

He reached out and took her hand, leading her to the very middle of the blanket. Once there, he held her in his arms, imprisoning her for a moment while he looked into her face.

Then he released her, but only so his hands could busy themselves, unbuttoning her shirt, then pushing it back off her shoulders to drop, carelessly discarded, on the ground.

Next he undid her bra and sent it downwards as well, then slid his fingers in the elasticised waistline of her shorts and tugged them off, hooking his fingers into her knickers at the same time so she could step out of both at once.

Kneeling before her, he unbuckled her sandals and slipped them off her feet, then he stood up, rested his hands on her shoulders and studied her for a moment.

'More a dryad than a fairy princess now!' he murmured. His brow wrinkled. 'Or do dryads need water? What spirits would you have in forests?'

Before she could reply, he bent his head and kissed her

on the lips, then touched his mouth to both her breasts in turn.

Fran felt her nipples harden, and desire arc like an electric current, tightening other tissues in her body as it prepared to welcome him.

'So, seductress, have your way with me,' he said, straightening up and holding out his arms—inviting her to strip him as he had stripped her.

Her fingers shaking with the strength of her increasing need, she managed to undo his shirt, but apparently her clumsiness was too much for him as well for he moved half a step away and pulled off his clothes with more speed than grace, casting garments and shoes in all directions in his haste.

And this time when he held out his arms she walked into them and nestled against him, pressing her body hard to his, needing the reassurance of their physical closeness more than she ever had before.

'Do we need to frolic naked through the trees first? Like me to chase and catch you?'

He whispered the words between deep and thirsty kisses, and Fran, unable to reply immediately, shook her head.

'I'm already caught,' she told him when she had enough breath to form words. Caught for ever, she added silently. Ensnared, trapped, and tangled in the love I have for you.

As despair sneaked through her defences once again, she kissed him more desperately, until need made her knees go weak and she forced them down so they could feast more easily on each other's bodies.

'Wanton woman!' Griff teased, when she needed more than feasting and took the initiative in their love-making. 'I thought we were here to look at Christmas trees.'

But he met and matched her passion with his own, so she was able to lose herself in the sensations and the fulfilment of their mutual need and for a while forget what lay ahead.

Griff fell asleep in her arms much later, and she peeled herself away from him, her body reluctant to leave his warmth. She dressed quickly, balled his shirt into a small pillow and tucked it under his head, then folded the blanket across his body to keep him warm.

And went to look at Christmas trees.

Griff picked his way through the forest, finally coming upon his wife on the far side of the small plantation. She was kneeling in the soft mulch, examining the disposition of the branches on what looked to him like a perfectly shaped tree.

'Found one you like?' he asked, and she looked up, as if surprised by his presence. Her cheeks reddened slightly, and he wondered if she was embarrassed by her uninhibited behaviour earlier.

Or as if he'd caught her thinking thoughts that weren't of him.

He swore at the suspicious entity that had taken up residence in his skull, and knelt beside her to have a better look at the chosen tree.

And the pink cheeks!

The confusion in her eyes suggested embarrassment, and he felt obliged to kiss away her fears, to hold her gently in his arms and tell her how much he'd enjoyed their woodland interlude.

'Not to mention your wantonness, my wife!' he added lightly. 'Made me realise I'll have to keep an eye on you in pine glades in the future.'

Wrong move?

Bad choice of words?

He felt her body lose its pliancy and a tremor pass across her skin.

'We should mark the tree so I know which one I've chosen,' she said, but the words were weak and shaky and he knew their woodland interlude had made things worse, not better.

'I'll tie my handkerchief around it,' he said, pulling the square of white from his pocket.

What he'd wanted to say had been What's wrong, Franny? But he sensed she wasn't any more ready to talk to him now than she had been when he'd first suggested they discuss things.

Yet she took his hand to walk back to their picnic place, and pressed her body against his so they moved as one.

The scented air filled his lungs and the stillness of the green glade was all about him. But his body swirled with turmoil and uncertainty, and the bleakness of his thoughts was casting longer shadows than the trees.

They ate their picnic, Fran doing her determined-chatter thing, covering topics from Christmas decorations to diphtheria epidemics. Griff ate sandwiches and cake, the food as interesting as sawdust on his tongue as he worried over the problem of what was happening in his marriage.

Then, as Fran stretched out to fill his teacup from the Thermos, a beam of sunshine, filtered down through the branches of the trees, struck gold lights in her hair, and his heart squeezed so painfully he thought he might be having an infarct.

Dear heaven! He couldn't let his marriage die. It might have begun in fun but it was now so very real to him. Necessary. Essential to his spirit, like air and water were to his body.

He sat up straighter, planning. Thinking of what had to be done to win her back.

For a start there was no way she was going to Toowoomba on her own.

Not with Ian Sinclair taking leave at the same time.

Billie Lloyd was coming to the party. He'd start with her.

And if he was going away, he'd have to sort out Melanie's problems first.

He drained his tea and threw the plastic cup back into the basket.

'Best be on our way!' he said briskly.

So many things to do. So little time.

Fran watched him bundle up the picnic things. So much for an idyllic day in the country. They'd made love, eaten, Griff had even slept, but now he wanted to be on the move again.

'I've got to see Melanie Miller this afternoon,' he added, as if that explanation should placate Fran rather than send her into a burning frenzy of jealousy.

She should be glad, she told herself as she followed him glumly back to the car. Even if darling Melanie *was* too old to give him the children he wanted, she'd do to fill any gap Fran's departure might happen to leave.

But his interest in her might blind him to more suitable women!

She argued the situation back and forth with herself all the way to town.

'Thanks for a lovely outing, Franny mine,' her erratic husband said as they pulled up back at home. He kissed her cheek then positively leapt out of the car.

Anxious, no doubt, to be with Melanie!

And the week didn't improve. Busy during the day, emergency calls at night, three long, tiring evenings spent at the council chambers, sticking needles into children who cried and adults who grumbled and complained about the necessity for booster shots.

In between, Fran decorated the house with her leaves and

garlands, transforming it into a red and green bower. The flowers would wait until Saturday, but the tree…

'Do you think we could go out to Ian's place at lunchtime and cut the tree?' she asked Griff on Friday morning.

'And bring it back home in the car?' he said. 'Hanging out of the boot? Have you any idea how big that tree is?'

Fran held out her hand at shoulder level and Griff laughed.

'I think you'll find it's twice that high. I've already spoken to Ian about it and explained where it is. His farmhand will be delivering it today, and Barney's dropping off a big pot—half a barrel, in fact—to stand it up in. They'll set it up for you.'

Fran was so relieved to have the problem of the tree delivery solved that she forgot about keeping her distance and threw her arms around him to give him a tight, hard hug.

'Thank you,' she said, and meant it, although her skin, denied the touch of his since their 'wanton' picnic, thought the embrace was something else and her arms were reluctant to let him go.

'We're already late for work,' Griff reminded her, although he didn't seem too committed to departure either.

Fran sighed, and moved reluctantly away. Tonight they'd be busy decorating the tree, tomorrow preparing for the party, tomorrow night exhausted, Sunday cleaning up and recovering, and on Monday she was leaving, if only temporarily this time.

But it would be the main break—the dislocation to their marriage which would make her eventual departure a foregone conclusion.

Again the air left her lungs in a deep, whooshing kind of sigh, this time attracting Griff's attention.

'I told you it was too much for you. All this party nonsense,' he said crossly, then he seemed to reconsider his reaction, for he kissed her lightly on the top of the head and added, 'Well, at least you can have a bit of a rest in Toowoomba. I had a quick glance through the programme and some of the lectures are so boring you could skip them without feeling any guilt at all.'

He gave her an enigmatic smile that made her wonder if he was looking forward to her departure for reasons of his own.

Melanie Miller?

Or was it to do with the phone conversation she'd overheard a couple of evenings earlier? One where she'd thought she'd caught the name 'Billie' and realised he'd been talking to his old girlfriend.

She'd had to be really firm with herself that evening, reminding herself that it was *her* plan after all, and that she should be pleased, not wrung out with jealousy.

'I'm off,' she told him, whisking out the back door before he could see the agony this 'doing the right thing' was causing her. 'See you later.'

Taking two cars, that was something else she'd instigated this week. After the drive out to Ian's farm, when she'd wanted to snuggle against her husband, she'd realised she couldn't rely on her mind to overcome her body's urges, especially in as intimate an area as the inside of a car. Being apart as often as possible, that was definitely the best policy.

'You've an early patient waiting for you.'

Meg greeted Fran with this information, and moved her head to indicate the waiting room.

The only patient in view was Melanie Miller, immaculate as ever.

'Mrs Miller? But she always sees Griff.'

'She asked specifically for you today,' Meg murmured. 'Do you want a few minutes before I send her in?'

The news that Melanie Miller wanted to see her made

Fran feel physically ill, but postponing the meeting wasn't going to help. In fact, she'd only feel sicker for longer.

'No, send her in,' she said glumly as an imaginary conversation with the older woman began to play itself over in her head. Actually, it was a replay of one she'd had before—one where a patient at the twenty-four-hour clinic had turned out to be one of Richard's lovers, coming to announce that she was pregnant and to point out it was Fran's duty to divorce her husband, leaving him free to marry the mother of his child.

Fran's stomach churned uneasily, but she fought the weakness, telling herself it was unlikely Mrs Miller was pregnant, though the rest of their consultation could easily go to script.

'Griff tells me he keeps patient confidentiality even from you, except in cases where it's necessary to consult.'

Fran took a moment to process the words when Mrs Miller's opening foray wasn't what she'd expected. She nodded to show she'd heard and opened Mrs Miller's file while she considered their meaning.

Mrs Miller, taking her silence as understanding, continued, 'So you don't know the background, but when he told me you were adopted and suggested I should talk to you, I realised that perhaps you'd have a better understanding of the situation and some inkling as to whether I'd do more harm than good.'

The woman was nervous—that explained the sudden outpouring of words. One portion of Fran's brain registered this while another was up in arms over Griff respecting the patient's confidentiality but telling all and sundry *her* life history.

Just wait until I get hold of him! This was good. Being angry—no, furious—with him would make leaving ever so much easier.

'Been so kind, so patient, spent so much time, his own

free time, with me, but he says he can't make the decision for me and I don't know what to do.'

Mrs Miller looked hopefully at her and Fran realised her patient had continued talking and she, the doctor, hadn't heard a single word.

She tried a smile. Mixed in with all her other confusion was a stupid sense of relief that Griff *had* been seeing Mrs Miller professionally.

'I'm sorry. I missed that. I was thinking. Wondering what me being adopted had to do with anything.'

Mrs Miller frowned at her.

'Perhaps if I start at the beginning,' she said. 'I was explaining about Jessica. About her being my birth daughter and giving her up for adoption. I always knew who'd adopted her, and when she was twenty-one I wrote to her parents to ask how they thought she would handle meeting me. If it was a good idea.'

Jessica!

'Jessica Drake?' Fran asked, remembering Griff's firm response when Fran had tried to include Mrs Miller as one of her recruits to help young Peter. 'Jessica's your birth daughter?'

If she hadn't been watching—in wonder more than anything else—Fran might have missed the tears that Mrs Miller blinked determinedly away.

'The family who'd adopted her didn't reply so I wrote again, and then again. Finally, the man rang up—her father—and said not to keep writing because...'

This time there were too many tears to blink away and Fran came around the desk and squatted down to put her arm around the woman's shoulders.

Let her cry.

'I'm sorry. I haven't even told Griff this. I told him the man said Jessica had left home and they didn't know where she was. But what he said was that he hadn't seen her for years but I'd be pleased to know she'd turned out a slut, just like her mother! He must have used that word to her, a teenager, barely more than a child. Used the word and either turned her out of the house or made her so miserable she ran away. Just when she needed someone.'

The hateful recollection brought more tears, while Fran thought of the wonderful couple who'd brought her up—who had nurtured her and praised her and encouraged her to be the best she could, yet had always been grateful to the woman who had borne her and given her up. They had spoken lovingly of her, and eventually had helped Fran look for her.

'She was pregnant?' Fran probed when the tears had given way to an occasional sniff. Sometimes it seemed everyone was pregnant but herself!

'Apparently, although the man didn't tell me that. And he had no idea where she'd gone so I had to drop the whole thing for a while. My husband had just been diagnosed with cancer. He had treatment and was ill for a long time. When he died, I was lost. Empty. We'd never had a child—the two of us. In the end, I decided I'd try to find her—my daughter.'

'How?' Fran demanded, although she knew the usual channels. She'd tried for years to find her mother that way, tried harder after the couple who had been her real parents had passed away.

'I hired a private detective to do all the paperwork. First he checked marriage records to make sure she hadn't changed her name, then he started on voting registers. When he told me he'd found her and gave me her address, I lost my courage. Didn't know what to do. She'd had one family who'd let her down. She could have been resentful of me for giving her up for adoption. I thought she might not want to see me, know me.'

'Yet you came here anyway,' Fran said quietly.

'I needed to see her. Needed to know she was all right.'

Fran nodded. She could understand that. In a way it was why she was working on Plans A and B. She needed to know Griff would be all right!

'And now?' she said gently.

'I'm stuck. At first I thought I'd write to her, ask if she wanted to see me, but then I wondered what I'd do if she didn't reply. Or wrote back to say no. Griff says I'm letting what might happen destroy me. I've been having panic attacks and he's been treating those, says I should see a specialist, but he's all I need at the moment. He's a very understanding man.'

Fran's heart scrunched its agreement, then she remembered she was angry with him.

'But he won't offer any opinion about me writing or not writing,' Mrs Miller continued. 'He says I have to decide that for myself, and be sure I can live with my decision. But how could I live with a decision that cuts off any hope for getting to know her?'

The fear in the woman's voice was real, and strong enough for Fran to forget any subsidiary thoughts and concentrate.

'Griff asked you to our pre-dinner party tomorrow night,' she said. 'Knowing Jessica would be there. That's hardly keeping out of things, letting you make the decision.'

'I begged him to, cried all over him, made a big issue of just getting to meet her socially.' There was a small pause then she added, 'I lied to him. Told him if I could just meet her once, properly, not in the pharmacy where she serves me like any other customer, I'd leave town, go away. File my name with all the agencies in case she ever wanted to find me, but leave her alone. I really thought if she could get to know me, even like me a little...'

'But it might be just the thing to get her back up,' Fran objected, wondering just how many tears Mrs Miller had shed before Griff had agreed to the daft proposal. 'She might see it as underhand.'

Piteous eyes looked into hers.

'I realise that now. I told Griff yesterday I wouldn't come to the party. He was relieved, but he was anxious about me. That's why he said I should talk to you.'

'What can I do?' Fran asked. 'My relationship with Jessica is purely professional. She's never mentioned to me that she's adopted. In fact, there's been an occasion recently when it could have come up and she said nothing.'

There was a long pause, during which Fran tried to figure out exactly what her patient wanted of her. She was way over time as well, and the patients with appointments would be lining up outside.

'Griff said you'd looked for your birth mother. I wondered if you ever talked about that. With your friends.' A strengthening of Mrs Miller's voice suggested they were reaching the crux of the visit. 'If you could mention it, perhaps in Jessica's hearing, at the party. Make it sound positive. Like something good to do.'

Fran frowned.

'That feels very manipulative to me,' she muttered.

'But only because people don't talk about it enough. Hundreds, perhaps thousands, of people are involved in searches for missing bits of their families any day of the year, but no one talks about it. The birth mother carries a load of guilt, the child a sackful of resentment. We're coming up to Christmas. A time for families to be together. Would it be such a bad subject to raise at your party?'

And on that note Mrs Miller rose from her chair, shouldered her handbag and stalked out the door.

Before Fran could fully assimilate the abrupt departure, Meg appeared, a pile of files in her hand. She dropped them on the desk and cocked an eyebrow at Fran.

'Upset her again, did you?' she asked, and Fran shook her head.

'I thought we were doing quite well,' she said. 'Then suddenly she's up and out of here like the devil himself was on her tail.'

'Well, with this lot waiting at the door, you won't have time to brood about it.'

Meg patted the files and headed for the door.

'Shall I send in number one?'

'Might as well,' Fran said, but she wondered how effective a doctor she'd be with so much else on her mind.

If ever there was a young woman who could do with some family support it was Jessica Drake. But was a family you didn't want worse than no family at all?

Fran greeted her next patient absently, then, with a supreme effort of will, put Mrs Miller's revelations out of her mind and concentrated on what had to be done right here and now.

Although the argument she was going to have with her husband when she got him on his own simmered nicely in her subconscious.

CHAPTER TEN

'How could you dump Mrs Miller on me like that? What can I possibly do to help the woman?'

Fran was standing on the stepladder, hanging a red bell on one of the topmost branches of the Christmas tree, and Griff, coming in from a couple of late appointments at the surgery, had been greeted by her anger.

So much for a cosy night alone, and his plans to spring the great surprise on her!

'Hey! If we're going to argue, come down to ground level,' he countered. 'It's not fair if you have a height advantage.'

'I'm serious,' she said. 'Talk about unprofessional behaviour.'

Aware of her anger, even without her endorsement, he was even more aware of her perilous perch, particularly as the ladder seemed to shake every time she moved on it.

Damned woman hadn't even made sure the feet were steady.

He stepped forward and reached out to take her arm.

'I know you're serious,' he said, 'but come down from there. You're giving me heart failure, swaying about like that. I'll get up the ladder and you can pass the pretties up and tell me where you want them. We'll talk as we work.'

Her arm stiffened with resistance but she climbed down, still grumbling at him.

'I don't see that it makes any difference who's on the ladder. What if you fall? What then?'

'The way you've been behaving lately, I'd have thought

you'd be pleased,' he said crossly. Nothing was working out today—nothing!

'Pleased to have you in hospital with a broken leg or cracked skull? Why on earth would I be pleased?'

She looked so lovely, frowning up at him, a bit of glitter stuck to her left cheek and small threads of tinsel caught in her golden hair.

'Let's start again,' he said. 'Good evening Fran. Sorry to be late home, but what with one thing and another…'

He bent and kissed her gently on the lips, then straightened to look into dark, drown-in brown eyes.

'Now, about Melanie. I hadn't realise she intended seeing you today. Nor did I send her to you for a solution. I did tell her you were adopted, because I thought you might have some insights to offer her about how an adopted child feels. Remember how suspicious we were about her early visits—how trivial they seemed?'

Fran nodded, though Griff sensed it was a reluctant agreement.

'Well, all those were excuses—first to meet both of us, then to decide I was most likely to be useful in her search as I'd been here longer and knew the townsfolk. It was ages before she actually mentioned why she'd come to town.'

He dropped another kiss on Fran's upturned lips.

'Then, when she did begin to talk, the admission, or confession or whatever you'd call it, really upset her. That's when she'd call and ask me to go around at night. Talking about it had brought back all the trauma of becoming pregnant, and her family's horrified reaction. The hiding and subterfuge! She was sent to a place for unmarried mothers and her friends were told she was overseas. Poor thing had to study travel guides so she could talk about where she'd been. Then, of course, when she eventually married and she and her husband didn't have children, she saw it as divine retribution of some kind!'

He watched his wife's soft pink mouth form into an O.

'I didn't understand just how hard it must have been for her,' Fran told him. 'When she came in, all she talked about was whether to write or not to write, then she asked me if I'd talk about being adopted in front of Jessica.'

Griff studied her face as she explained, and realised he hadn't considered Fran's background when puzzling over their recent estrangement. Could being adopted make a woman want her own children more badly? Would it make her less likely to go for adoption herself?

He felt physically ill as he considered what might lie ahead. Especially if *he* proved to be the problem in the failure-to-conceive scenario!

'And would you?' he asked, when he realised from the silence it must be his turn to speak. 'Talk about it in front of Jessica?'

'Well, it's nothing to be ashamed of,' his wife said stoutly. 'There's no real reason why I shouldn't. And if it might help Jessica...'

She sounded so forlorn he had to put his arms around her, and hold her tightly against his body.

'So what's worrying you? Apart from your husband betraying your past?'

She wriggled uncomfortably, then mumbled into his shirt.

'I understand why you did that.'

As an apology it wasn't bad!

'But talking about it,' she continued, giving a little shrug, 'in such a planned way. In front of Jessica. It seems manipulative.'

He rocked her gently for a moment then said, 'Isn't a lot of what we do manipulative? Don't we work our way around awkward situations? Try to find a solution that's likely to be acceptable to each particular patient rather than order them to do this or take that?'

Another nod, and the warm pliant body in his arms snuggled closer.

Sensing victory, he dropped a kiss on the tangled hair and was about to move into more serious seduction when the front doorbell pealed.

Fran untwined herself from her husband's arms and went to answer it.

A tall slim brunette was standing on her doorstep.

A tall, slim, undeniably beautiful brunette.

'J-Josie?'

Fran stuttered out the name, suddenly not sure about either Plan A or Plan B.

'Hi,' the vision of loveliness said. 'You must be Fran. I'm Sheila's cousin, Josie, and it's wonderful of you to ask me to stay. You've no idea how much I've been longing for some real country fun.'

She held out her hand to Fran, then sauntered in, a large soft leather bag slung across her shoulder apparently her only luggage.

'And you must be Griff,' she added, holding out the hand again to Griff, while Fran tried to find her tongue, work out what to say in welcome.

'Oh, look, a tree! It's real! How wonderful. May I help decorate it? Do you have an angel for the top? My parents have been having Christmas dinner at a hotel recently and it's not the same. They don't decorate the house or anything. I guess they think now I'm grown up, they don't need to. Do you two have kids that you've gone to so much trouble? I absolutely love the garlands.'

She dropped her bag, then riffled through the box of decorations, found a golden ball and climbed up the ladder to hang it. Josie had made herself at home.

Fran stifled a giggle as she realised she didn't have to

say anything. She slanted a glance at her husband who was staring at their guest with a shell-shocked expression.

Perhaps Plan A will work after all, Fran thought glumly as her mood shifted abruptly.

'Why don't you and Josie do the tree, while I fix us something to eat?' she said.

Griff gabbled something, but she walked away, needing the privacy of the kitchen so she could have a little cry and remind herself why this was the right thing to do.

By continuing to tell herself it was the only way to go, Fran managed to get through the evening. In fact, there were even times when she enjoyed it, mainly because Josie's enthusiasm for the simple fun of decorating a Christmas tree was contagious.

The only problem had been the arrival of Ian Sinclair, who'd come to see if he could help and had to be invited to join them. Though later, when Fran caught Griff scowling at the genial vet, she felt her heartache intensify. The only reason for that scowl would be that the love-at-first-sight scenario had worked after all, and as Ian seemed to be vying for Josie's attention Griff was upset.

Well, you don't have to watch them fight over her, Fran told herself and, after showing Josie the guest bedroom and bathroom, she used the excuse of extreme tiredness and retired to bed.

And she *was* tired, though sleep seemed far away. Especially when Griff followed her, sat on the edge of the bed and brushed his hand across her hair.

'Poor darling. You've knocked yourself out with all this festivity. Can I get you something?'

Like a new heart?

She shook her head and curled into a tighter ball, then decided she didn't want him worried—and, furthermore, didn't want Ian staking any claims on their guest.

She uncurled and flashed him one of her best and brightest smiles.

'I'm fine, just tired,' she said. 'Sorry to leave you with entertaining the guests, but if I don't get some sleep I'll be even more useless tomorrow night.'

Griff bent and kissed her on the cheek, then left the room, but outside the door he hovered, concern for Fran weighing heavily on his shoulders. This tiredness was worrying. He'd have to talk her into having blood tests done—just to be sure there was no underlying cause. Anaemia perhaps. A psychologist might suggest it was an avoidance procedure. Symptomatic of an underlying concern.

Like not falling pregnant?

He thought gloomily of the tests he was determined to take, and wondered if he'd have the courage to make the right decision—for Fran if not himself—if his fears were proved correct.

The following day was chaotic, but by five o'clock Fran was satisfied all was in order and she went upstairs to shower and dress. Josie was in the kitchen, swapping recipes with Patty, and while Fran knew she should be pleased the young woman was domesticated enough to be interested in cooking, the leaden feeling in her chest made her wonder if she had the strength to go through with her plans—no matter how much she loved Griff.

Love demands some sacrifice!

She repeated the words like some litany of faith, but they made her feel worse, not better. In fact, the very thought of life without Griff made her feel physically ill.

She stripped off her clothes and dumped them in the laundry hamper. She'd have to wash tomorrow. That mundane thought, and other domestic plans, got her through the shower, back to the bedroom, and into the fire-engine red dress she'd bought especially for the dance.

'Wow!'

The admiring exclamation brought her spinning around to see her husband standing in the doorway.

His eyes gleamed with what looked like admiration, but the puckering of the skin between his eyebrows suggested something else.

'Mind you, I'm not sure I want the male half of this town seeing you in it. It's…'

Fran looked down at herself. From her viewpoint, there did seem to be a lot of creamy breast on view.

'Too bare?'

Blue eyes skimmed up and down, then up again, increasing her nervousness and uncertainty.

'Not really.'

'You don't like it?' Insecurity joined the blend of emotions jostling for supremacy.

'No, it's great!'

'Boy! It sure sounds that way,' Fran muttered, as the lukewarm tone made a mockery of the words and frayed her nerves to irritation. 'If it looks dreadful, for heaven's sake, tell me. I do have other things I can wear.'

He stepped into the room and shut the door, then came closer.

'It looks great, Franny,' he said softly. 'Makes you look very curvy. Sexy!'

He groaned and shook his head, then grinned at her.

'Would you believe I feel jealous of my own wife?'

'Jealous of me?' The words made no sense. 'In that I might look better than you?'

He took another step towards her and reached out to touch the shadowed cleft between her breasts.

'Jealous that other men might look at you. Be attracted to you. Want you.'

Deep in Fran's heart a tiny flicker of hope melted an

atom of the lead, but she quickly squelched the idea she might be more than a wife of convenience to Griff.

'That should make you feel good, not bad,' she told him, trying for lightness to waylay the silly hope. 'Something to do with the pack leader getting his pick of the women. With me looking halfway decent, and Josie by your side as well, you'll be king of the kids tonight.'

But the look in Griff's eyes told her it went beyond a joke, and as he turned away towards the bathroom she wondered how it was possible to know someone as long as she'd known Griff yet not know how he felt.

With a sigh, she turned to her dressing-table and surveyed the array of make-up she rarely used. Josie had a way of making hers look completely natural, yet somehow highlighting her good features like her eyes and lips. Using the bones of her face as a guide, she'd explained to Fran during a woman-to-woman chat over the lunch dishes.

Fran dabbed and brushed and coloured, then sat back, not entirely displeased with the result.

'You look beautiful!'

Once again her husband took her by surprise, coming to stand behind her, studying her 'new' face in the mirror.

'Tricks of the trade, thanks to Josie,' Fran said lightly, for these compliments from Griff were throwing her off balance.

'No. It's more than that,' Griff said, and he bent to kiss her on the shoulder. 'It's inner goodness, Franny mine!'

Franny mine!

The expression, said so tenderly, made her eyes water, and, knowing all her good work with powder and paint was about to be undone, she sniffed loudly, slapped his wrist and told him he'd be late if he didn't get moving.

She whisked out of the room.

Griff watched her go. Watched the lush curves of her body beneath the shimmer of red. And while she might be sashaying sexily around in red, looking so spectacular he'd been tempted to lie and tell her the dress didn't suit her, there was still something gravely amiss with his wife.

He hadn't missed the tears that had welled when he'd kissed her. He added that to previous diagnoses. Weepy as well as tired all the time. Emotional response to a hormonal overload. Could she possibly be pregnant?

Not telling him?

Not know?

This idea was so astounding he had to sit down on the bed to handle it. Counted back. No! Not possible.

'Fantastic party!' Griff coiled his arm around Fran's waist. 'Only problem is, no one's going to want to leave to go on to the dinner-dance.'

'I don't know what's so fantastic about it,' Fran grumbled above the noise of background music and people chatting to each other.

'Everyone's getting on really well.' Griff murmured the words against her ear, making her tingle in a most unnecessary way. 'And isn't it great about Bill and Billie?'

Fran detached herself from her husband's arm and scowled at him. She could hardly deny that reconciliation was a good thing, but the party had begun badly when Billie had arrived, coming gaily up the garden path with Bill in tow.

'We're courting again, would you believe?' she'd brayed at Fran, who'd had trouble dredging up a smile, let alone enthusiasm. 'Such fun. Going away together like this feels almost illicit!'

Reassuring herself that she had other fish to fry—or women to offer up to Griff—Fran had managed to say the right things.

Then Ian had turned up minus his sister, who'd fled back

to the city after *her* boyfriend had phoned to complain of being lonely.

And as for Josie…

'I don't think it's going well at all,' Fran told her husband as disappointment at the death rattles of her plan overcame her common sense. 'Look at the way Josie's flirting with Ian. Honestly! The girl's got no class, carrying on like that with someone she's just met.'

'Hey, just because they hit it off immediately, it's not necessarily bad. Boy! Even I noticed the chemistry between the two of them kick in last night, and you know how blind and deaf I usually am to that kind of thing.'

Fran scowled again. Over in a corner, Jessica Drake was flirting with one of the school teachers. Melanie Miller hadn't come, but earlier in the evening Jessica, learning from Josie via Sheila that Fran was adopted, had cornered Fran to ask how to go about finding her birth mother.

Fran had told her the various channels she could use, then said, 'It mightn't be as hard as you think, Jessica. Have a good think about it and make sure it's what you want, then come and see me—or see Griff. We'll help you out from there.'

Jill, the last hope, was firmly attached to the other school teacher. Not only attached but wearing his ring. And Janet, who might have done in a pinch, was obviously besottedly in love with her newly returned husband, refusing to be parted from him for even a minute.

'So stop worrying,' Griff said, cuddling her closer and reminding her how good things had been between them. 'Just relax and enjoy yourself. Have you got your bags packed for Toowoomba?'

'Can't wait to get rid of me, can you?' Fran said grumpily. 'A few weeks ago you were all up in arms because I'd decided to go, and now you're practically pushing me out the door. I don't need to go tomorrow. I can leave early Monday morning and still get there in time for registration.'

He kissed her lightly on the cheek.

'Leaving tomorrow will give you an extra day to relax. After all the work you've done…' he waved his hand to the beautifully decorated room, glowing with the reds and greens she'd combined so artfully '…you deserve a break.'

'I'll have to clean up here,' she muttered, annoyed that he seemed so anxious to get rid of her, although it had been part of Plan B for her to depart as soon as possible.

'Leave it to Josie. And Patty said she'd come in,' he reminded her, then added, in a voice that made her wonder just what was going on, 'And me, of course.'

'Come along, everyone. Time to move on.'

Meg's husband Roy was one of the team leaders of the fire service and he waved his arm towards the door.

People began to troop out, calling thanks back to Fran and Griff and see-you-laters to each other.

'Do we have to go on to the dinner?' Griff asked, when all the guests had departed, Ian taking Josie in his car.

A sudden wave of exhaustion tempted Fran to say no, but she knew there'd be talk, and if things went the way she thought they would there'd be enough of that later.

Although, given the failure of Plans A and B, she'd better come up with a C pretty quickly, or leaving Griff at New Year would be impossible.

Deciding it was all too confusing, she allowed her husband to usher her out of the house, then, using the excuse that they had so little time left together, she put all thought of Plans A, B or C out of her mind and gave herself up to enjoyment of the evening.

Which wasn't hard when Griff seemed to feel he'd done all the socialising necessary for one night and kept her to himself, dancing close, and slowly, making her feel cherished and secure.

Loved, almost!

'Come on, come on, lazybones, up and out of there.'

'Go away. It's Sunday and if I want to stay in bed all day I can. Ian's taking Josie out to his farm so I don't even have to entertain our house guest.'

Fran burrowed her head deeper into the pillow.

'Well, just tell me which of these two sweaters you want to take. You know how cool it can be in Toowoomba at this time of the year.'

The question was sufficiently bizarre for Fran to raise her head and open eyes which protested at the light.

'What are you doing?' she demanded when she saw Griff standing at the foot of the bed, her half-packed case open on the dressing-table stool and two cardigans, one a fine-knit black, the other a pale beige, dangling from his fingers.

'You're packing for me?' She shot bolt upright in the bed. 'Are you so desperate to get rid of me?'

Her suspicions awoke before he could answer.

It *had* to be Melanie Miller! In spite of the explanations about Jessica, there *must* be something going on. All the other candidates—her hand-picked few—had failed, but if Griff was infatuated by Melanie, it wouldn't matter anyway.

'Which one?' Griff said in a long-suffering voice that husbands seemed to acquire during the marriage ceremony.

'I'm not going!' Fran heard herself say, then she quivered as she realised how close she'd come to adding, She's not right for you!

But Melanie wasn't. Apart from not being able to give him children, she wouldn't make Griff comfortable. Fran knew this at some instinctive level where love and knowledge co-existed.

And if he was going to be stuck with someone who couldn't breed, then he could damned well be stuck with her, Fran, who loved him more than life itself. Would Melanie Miller have given him up for love? Fran didn't think so!

'I've changed my mind!' she announced, sitting up in bed and crossing her arms. Ready for a fight. 'I'll call the conference committee tomorrow and tell them I can't make it.'

'Then we'll go somewhere else,' Griff announced. 'Come on, choose a cardigan and get out of bed. I want to throw the sheets into the washing machine. Patty's sending one of her helpers over to tidy the house, and Mum's coming down to supervise.'

The 'we'll' in the first sentence threw Fran momentarily, but not as much as the final bit of information.

'Coming down to supervise what?' she managed to say, but demands weren't as strong when you were totally confused.

'Cleaning up after the party, making up the bed again, clearing a few things from our bedroom cupboards so Bill and Billie can hang up their stuff.'

'Bill and Billie?' Fran shook her head and looked piteously at her husband. 'Is this conversation supposed to be making sense?'

He smiled at her and came to sit down on the bed.

'It was a surprise,' he said, taking her in his arms and brushing his hand down her tangled mane of hair. 'Only, the way I'd imagined it, you had your bags already packed to go to Toowoomba today, and when you went out to the car to drive off I was going to get in as well and you'd ask what I thought I was doing, and I'd tell you we were running away together. A second honeymoon, although we didn't really have a first one.'

Fran replayed this explanation in her mind, and found tears spurting as the word 'honeymoon' recurred.

'I'm crying again,' she mumbled against Griff's warm

chest. 'I don't know what's wrong with me. I haven't cried this much since my parents died.'

She took the handkerchief he offered and mopped up the tears, blew her nose, then straightened so she could look into his face.

'But I can't go on a honeymoon with you, Griff, darling.' The tears came back in full flow but she battled on. 'I'm leaving you.'

She sobbed out the final words against his neck, and clasped her arms so tightly around his body it was a wonder he could breathe.

Oh, he could breathe all right. Not only breathe but move, shooting up off the bed as if her words had burnt him. Pacing now, back and forth, glaring at her. And finding enough air to yell as well.

'Leaving me? What on earth do you mean, you're leaving me? You can't leave me, Franny. I love you!'

She was trying to assimilate this bombshell when he sent another shock-wave through her.

'And if you're worried about this not conceiving thing, then we can adopt. Or try IVF if you want your own child. If my sperm's no good, you can use someone else's. It won't bother me, I promise you that, Fran.'

He'd stopped pacing and was kneeling by the bed now, his hand grasping hers as he peered anxiously into her face. His skin was pale, his eyes tormented, and the love she felt for him was breaking her heart.

'You think it's your fault I'm not pregnant?' she demanded. 'Oh, Griff, how could you torture yourself that way? As if it matters to me if we have children or not.'

'Then why this talk of leaving me? Why, Fran?'

She hung her head, let her hair fall to hide her eyes, then realised how stupid they both had been. How daft her plan to set him up with someone else had been.

Especially if he loved her. Had he really said that? Said

the words? She looked up, met his eyes and tried to ask the question that was in her heart.

But her lips were trembling too much, and her heart pounding too hard.

'You married me to have your children,' she said instead. 'A Christmas present for your mother, if I remember rightly.' She hesitated then put her fear into words. 'I think it's me. I finally put together a lot of symptoms and came up with endometriosis.'

She shrugged her shoulders to hide the pain this knowledge had cost her.

'And I love you too much to keep you tied to me if I can't fulfil my part of the bargain. So I thought someone younger, healthy—'

'You invited all those people here last night to set me up? To offer me a choice of future wives?'

Griff was on his feet and yelling again. Fran wondered if Josie had already left, if Patty's helper was here, then decided it didn't matter. All she'd tried to do was help.

'Well, you took long enough to get married the first time,' Fran snapped right back at him, enjoying the slow burn of anger where before there'd been only pain. 'I was worried, if I left you to your own devices, it might be years before you got around to it and you're not getting any younger and your mother isn't getting any healthier!'

'You're saying you did this for me?' He halted his pacing long enough to glare at her, then he threw up his arms in disgust and continued wearing out the carpet.

'Did it never occur to you to wonder why I took so long to get married? Did it?'

The pacing stopped again and he leant across the bed so he could do a close-up of his fury.

'Because someone else had married the only girl I ever wanted, that's why!' he stormed. 'OK, so I mightn't have realised it right away—in fact, it wasn't until Mum said something recently that it all clicked into place—but *you* must have known,' he finished. 'Aren't women supposed to know these things?'

Fran rubbed her eyes and massaged her temples.

Was Griff saying he'd always been in love with her?

Surely not.

Wouldn't she have known?

Guessed?

With Griff and his reputation for womanising?

No way!

'What are women supposed to know?' she asked him, determined to clear the matter up now they'd got this far. 'What am I supposed to know?'

'That I love you, damn it!' he yelled, storming around the room now, his arms flying every which way like some mad tenor in a very dramatic opera.

'Oh, I think we all realised that some time ago,' a quiet voice interjected. 'May I come in or will you yell at me as well?'

Eloise peered cautiously around the partly opened door.

'Only if you can make this woman see some sense,' Griff told her. 'She's been talking about leaving me, would you believe?'

'Well, if you often carry on the way you have been this morning, I wouldn't blame her,' Eloise said calmly. 'Fortunately, Josie's lived in Italy and has seen temperament in action, and I was so pleased to see you jolted out of your comfort zone that I enjoyed the performance.'

She peered anxiously at Fran.

'Are you all right, darling?'

By now totally lost, it was all Fran could do to nod.

'Good,' Eloise said. 'Then I'll go down and make you a nice cup of tea. I'll get Josie to bring it up. Twice up the stairs might be too much excitement for my heart.'

Concern for her patient brought Fran leaping out of bed.

'Now where are you going?' Griff demanded as she hurtled towards the door.

'To check out your mother. She shouldn't be put under pressure, you know that!'

Griff caught her and halted her headlong flight.

'My mother is fine,' he said firmly. 'I looked at her—good colour in her lips, a twinkle in her eye. My mother is having more fun than she's had for months. But this is about you and me, Franny. About me loving you, not letting you leave me, about me being reasonably certain I couldn't live without you.'

He released her, stepped back and ran his fingers through his hair in a distracted manner.

'Would you believe I was even jealous of the way you smiled at the twins? Even wondered, for one ghastly minute, if I'd be jealous of any child you and I might have?'

Fran sighed. Somehow the conversation had come full circle and sadness was again creeping into her heart.

'But that's what all of this is about, Griff,' she reminded him. 'Children!'

She paused, then added softly. 'It's why you married me!'

He echoed her sigh and drew her gently into his arms.

'Don't you understand, Fran. It's why I *thought* I married you. The excuse I used because to acknowledge I loved you was too much for me to handle.'

He tilted up her head and kissed her on the lips.

'Let's forget about the children thing—talk about that some other time—and concentrate on you and me. I love you, Franny, more than I can ever say, but if you'll stay with me, maybe I can show you just how much, every day, in every way.'

She eased back far enough to look up into his eyes.

'Are you saying we'll never argue? That you'll never roar at me?'

He grinned at her.

'Only when you're being *extremely* stupid!' he said grimly. 'Leaving me, indeed. I nearly had a heart attack myself!'

He kissed her again, a long, lingering kiss that sealed his declaration of love.

'But we could start working on those children if you like. What if you decide which sweater then have a shower while I finish packing? If we're going to put our hearts and souls into the effort, I'd prefer to be somewhere where my mother isn't.'

Which reminded Fran.

'I've made an appointment to see a specialist while I'm in Toowoomba and have a check-for problems, possibly a laparoscopy,' she admitted.

Griff chuckled.

'We're a matched pair for stupidity,' he told her. 'I've arranged to have a sperm count!'

Downstairs, Eloise heard their laughter, and smiled to herself. It was good for lovers to be able to laugh together.

EPILOGUE

THE specialist Jeff Jervis had recommended greeted them warmly.

'I love to see couples coming in together. Back when I began specialising men were beginning to attend the actual birth but most of them wouldn't be seen dead in an O and G office.'

Griff shifted from one foot to another. Fran guessed that, after running the gauntlet of the pregnant women in the waiting room, he was also wishing he were somewhere else.

Holding tightly to his hand, she explained the reason for the visit.

'A year isn't long in the conception stakes these days,' the doctor said gently, 'certainly not long enough to be panicking about infertility.'

Griff's fingers pressed against hers, an I-told-you-so message.

'Well, let's have a look at you.'

He half drew the curtain in front of his couch, giving her minimum space to strip and pull on one of the loose, thigh-length robes he provided for his patients.

He was thorough, Fran realised when the examination began. External, and starting with her breasts.

But as he palpated her abdomen he seemed to hesitate. 'Tell me again about your symptoms—the ones you've added up to endometriosis.'

Fran went through her cramps and back pain, heavy bleeding at times.

'And recently? Has the heavy bleeding continued?'

Fran's turn to frown as she tried to think. She'd been so distraught lately she hadn't really considered it.

'No. In fact, light but irregular.'

The man began to smile, and then to chuckle.

He called to Griff who stood up and joined him, peering down at Fran's prone body.

'Feel here,' he said to Griff, who went very pale. He'd missed the smile and chuckle and was no doubt imagining he'd feel some gross mass in his wife's abdomen.

'Go ahead,' the specialist urged, while a reason for the strange behaviour began to filter into Fran's consciousness.

Griff's look of wonder told her more.

'You're pregnant!' he said in most accusing tones.

'Well, *I* didn't know!' Fran retorted. 'Anyway, I can't be. I've still been having my cycle…' She paused and considered if that was actually true. 'Well, signs of it,' she muttered, afraid to believe the good news. 'Enough to make me think—'

'You're pregnant!' Griff repeated himself, but this time the words were loud, triumphant, encased with joy and laughter as he reached for Fran and helped her to sit up, then hugged her tightly.

He began to laugh.

'And here we were, you convinced you had endometriosis and I'm making appointments for sterility tests. It's like Mrs Robertson and the dog.'

Griff's laughter and the cryptic statement diverted Fran momentarily.

'People keep talking about Mrs Robertson. What's the story?'

He hugged her again.

'It happened when I first took over the practice. Typical new broom, I changed Mrs Robertson's heart tablets. Anyway, she was doing really well and I was congratulating her and myself when her dog had puppies.'

Fran closed her eyes to see if the story made any more sense that way.

'So?' she demanded, when the test had failed.

'The dog shouldn't have been pregnant. Because she was too young, Ian had given Mrs Robertson a script for the canine version of the Pill, but Mrs Robertson had mixed the two in her medicine cabinet and she'd been taking the dog's contraceptive pills and giving the dog her heart tablets.'

Fran had to smile, but she shook her head at the same time.

'That's the most ridiculous story I've ever heard, and I have no idea why you should be thinking about it now.'

'You asked me to tell it,' Griff reminded her. 'And you're pregnant. There's some connection. Isn't there?'

He turned to the specialist for confirmation, but Fran had stopped listening to his nonsense.

Inside her heart, hope was waiting to unfurl, but the doubts and pressures of recent weeks refused to be allayed. She was afraid to believe the miracle had happened.

'It's not possible,' she said firmly, addressing herself to her husband before he got too carried away with this idea. 'If you can feel it, it's advanced enough for me to have had some symptoms by now.' She felt her breasts. 'They're not sore. I haven't been sick.'

Well, she had been feeling queasy on and off, but she'd thought that had been to do with leaving Griff. Who was chatting to the specialist about ultrasounds, but obviously listening enough to hear her objections.

'Of course you've been displaying symptoms,' he argued. 'Mood swings, tears from my most untearful Franny, tired all the time. I did wonder!'

'You did not!' Fran retorted, struggling to her feet so she could argue more forcibly. 'If you did, why—?'

'Hey, kids!' the specialist intervened, literally stepping

between them. 'I thought the reason for this visit was concern about infertility, and now you've discovered it doesn't exist, at least not for the two of you, shouldn't you be happy?'

Fran looked at Griff, at the sheen of excitement in his blue eyes, the look of awed wonder on his face.

'Oh, we are,' she said softly, and reached out towards her husband.

'Very, very happy,' he said gruffly, and he folded her into his arms.

As their lips met, Fran heard the curtain rattle along the track.

'Two minutes!' They heard the disembodied voice of the man they'd just met. 'I've patients waiting, and you're due for an ultrasound, Mrs Dr Griffiths.'

An hour later, they were done. The cheerful nurse in the ultrasound rooms was waving a print from the machine in the air to dry it.

'You want a copy?' she asked, and Fran smiled at her.

'We certainly do,' she said. 'And could you gift-wrap it?'

'Gift-wrap it?' The nurse and Griff repeated the question in unison, but it was to Griff Fran turned.

'Isn't that the idea?' she said. 'Grandchildren for your mother? The perfect Christmas present?'

He groaned and took her in his arms again, oblivious to their audience.

'I can't believe I did that, asked you that way. That I was so stupid as to allow you to think...'

'It's over now,' Fran said gently. 'And has ended up for the best. The very best!'

He kissed her lightly on the lips, then raised his head.

'Yes, gift-wrapped, please,' he told the nurse, and, that settled, he turned his attention to more pressing matters, like finishing the kiss.

'I love you, Fran,' he whispered. 'Always and for ever. Truly, madly and deeply.'

And Fran smiled. 'You see, it did happen for you after all,' she said softly.

MILLS & BOON®

Makes any time special™

Mills & Boon publish 29 new titles every month. Select from...

Modern Romance™   **Tender Romance**™

Sensual Romance™

Medical Romance™   **Historical Romance**™

MAT2

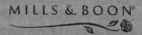

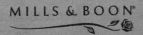

FREE
4 BOOKS
AND A SURPRISE GIFT!

We would like to take this opportunity to thank you for reading this Mills & Boon® book by offering you the chance to take FOUR more specially selected titles from the Medical Romance™ series absolutely FREE! We're also making this offer to introduce you to the benefits of the Reader Service™ —

★ FREE home delivery
★ FREE monthly Newsletter
★ FREE gifts and competitions
★ Exclusive Reader Service discounts
★ Books available before they're in the shops

Accepting these FREE books and gift places you under no obligation to buy; you may cancel at any time, even after receiving your free shipment. Simply complete your details below and return the entire page to the address below. *You don't even need a stamp!*

YES! Please send me 4 free Medical Romance books and a surprise gift. I understand that unless you hear from me, I will receive 6 superb new titles every month for just £2.40 each, postage and packing free. I am under no obligation to purchase any books and may cancel my subscription at any time. The free books and gift will be mine to keep in any case.

MOZEC

Ms/Mrs/Miss/Mr ....Initials ....
BLOCK CAPITALS PLEASE

Surname ....

Address ....

....

....Postcode ....

Send this whole page to:
UK: FREEPOST CN81, Croydon, CR9 3WZ
EIRE: PO Box 4546, Kilcock, County Kildare (stamp required)

Offer valid in UK and Eire only and not available to current Reader Service subscribers to this series. We reserve the right to refuse an application and applicants must be aged 18 years or over. Only one application per household. Terms and prices subject to change without notice. Offer expires 30th June 2001. As a result of this application, you may receive further offers from Harlequin Mills & Boon Limited and other carefully selected companies. If you would prefer not to share in this opportunity please write to The Data Manager at the address above.

Mills & Boon® is a registered trademark owned by Harlequin Mills & Boon Limited.
Medical Romance™ is being used as a trademark.